# THAT TENDER FEELING

# THAT TENDER FEELING

Dorothy Vernon

Chivers Press · Thorndike Press
Bath, England   Waterville, Maine USA

This Large Print edition is published by Chivers Press, England, and by Thorndike Press, USA.

Published in 2002 in the U.K. by arrangement with the author c/o Juliet Burton Literary Agency.

Published in 2002 in the U.S. by arrangement with Juliet Burton Literary Agency.

U.K. Hardcover  ISBN 0–7540–7433–1  (Chivers Large Print)
U.S. Softcover   ISBN 0–7862–4542–5  (Nightingale Series Edition)

The text of this Large Print edition is unabridged.
Other aspects of the book may vary from the original edition.

Set in 16 pt. New Times Roman.

Printed in Great Britain on acid-free paper.

**British Library Cataloguing in Publication Data available**

**Library of Congress Cataloging-in-Publication Data**

Vernon, Dorothy.
      That tender feeling / Dorothy Vernon.
          p.  cm.
      ISBN 0–7862–4542–5 (lg. print : sc : alk. paper)
      1. Yorkshire (England)—Fiction. 2. Women cooks—Fiction.
      3. Large type books. I. Title.
      PR6072.E737 T47 2002
      823'.914—dc21
                                                          2002075215

# CHAPTER ONE

The arrival of the solicitor's letter containing the news that Aunt Miranda had bequeathed Hawthorn Cottage to Ros in her will brought its share of friction. Ros's fiancé, Jarvis Trent, thought the only sensible course was to put it up for sale. He had pointed out that if it had been within easy traveling distance, it might have had a certain appeal as a country retreat; but it was so far away, buried way up in Yorkshire, that it wasn't feasible to hang on to it. Ros wanted to keep it, even though she knew that Jarvis was right and she was being impractical. She had a nostalgic yearning to recapture the happy days of her childhood that had been spent under Aunt Miranda's roof. A roof that now leaked.

The electrical wiring was pronounced unsafe, and the plumbing, so investigation revealed, had finally surrendered to old age. In the end, common sense prevailed, and Ros reluctantly bowed to her fiancé's judgment and agreed to let the cottage go.

On reaching that decision, Ros discovered that no one wanted to buy an inconveniently situated cottage in such a deplorable state. So, once again, Jarvis chipped in with his opinion.

'Unless you want to give the cottage away, it might be as well to invest in repairs and modernization.'

She had put the sale of the cottage in the hands of a real estate agent, and as the agent's recommendation merely endorsed Jarvis's advice, Ros gave instructions for the necessary work to be carried out.

The day she received notification that the work had been completed was also the day she was unavoidably held up. She phoned Glenis, her roommate, explaining that she hadn't a chance of getting home by the time Jarvis arrived to collect her for their date. Would Glenis be a love and keep him happy until she arrived? Glenis obligingly said she would. Ros wasn't as delayed as she had anticipated, and she walked in to find Jarvis being entertained in a way that was rather too warm for her to stomach. They had their arms wrapped round one another and were kissing passionately. It wasn't a light, impulsive kiss that could be forgiven; they were making a heavy session of it.

She looked at them in stunned disbelief; then her volatile temper surged up out of the grip of shock, and she let fly with her tongue, blasting them to high heaven.

She couldn't believe it of Jarvis. She swallowed hard, endeavoring to compose herself, expecting Jarvis to stutter out some abject words of apology. Instead, he turned on her and lashed back, in bitter accusation, 'That was a sneaky entrance.'

She gaped at him in astonishment. 'I've always had a soft tread. I didn't think I'd need to come in stamping my feet and making a lot of noise.'

If he'd looked the tiniest bit shame-faced, perhaps the outcome would have been different. But he jutted his chin at her; his whole stance was belligerent. 'It's no more than you should expect. Hasn't it ever occurred to you that if there isn't enough warmth on the home front, a man will warm his hands elsewhere?'

Glenis had at least had the decency to disappear into her bedroom, and so only Jarvis witnessed the deep blush staining Ros's cheeks, the held-back brightness in her eyes. Their lovemaking had always been temperate. They had never embraced with the total abandonment of the clinch she had just burst in on. Yet she had felt secure in Jarvis's affection, content to let the deeper passion come later. It wasn't a viewpoint that Jarvis shared, but he'd seemed to have come to terms with it.

Miserably, she twisted her engagement ring from her finger and held it out to him. She wasn't being melodramatic. Even only half assessed in her mind, the action seemed the only thing to do, despite the pain it caused her.

'It surely doesn't have to come to this, Ros?'

The way he looked at her was very nearly her undoing. She had known Jarvis for four years, at first hankering after him like a schoolgirl with an outsized crush on someone who was totally out of reach. He hadn't gotten around to noticing her in the way she'd wanted to be noticed until shortly after her twentieth birthday. Two years later, just six months ago, coinciding with the time her career took a sharp upward turn—one piece of good fortune really did seem to attract another—he had asked her to marry him, and she had felt as if the sky had opened and dropped a handful of stars into her lap. Two of them had been in her eyes as she had uttered a breathless yes. She didn't want it to end like that. She still loved him. Love is a hardy little plant that doesn't wither at the first bad spell. However, his infidelity, in her own flat with her own roommate, had killed something else that merits equal importance when contemplating marriage, and that was trust. Perhaps he hadn't killed it off at that, but merely stunted it. She needed time to tell.

'Let me think about it, Jarvis. Meanwhile, take your ring back.'

'You can't mean this, Ros. You're taking one tiny incident and enlarging it out of all sense of proportion.'

'One incident, Jarvis? I think not.'

At that, he had the grace to look away, but he stood his ground, not offering to leave. Having failed to bring her around, he decided to let his fingers take up the battle. They reached forward to stroke down the tautness of her cheek before she realized what he was about or had time to move away.

'No, Jarvis, not that way,' she said, avoiding the more dangerous pursuit of his arms.

She couldn't bear to let him touch her, not with what she had just witnessed still burning a hole in her mind. Even if she forgave Jarvis eventually, she didn't think she would ever be able to erase that scene from her thoughts.

At last, he went. The moment the door closed behind him, Glenis emerged from her room. In Jarvis's presence, she had looked ill at ease; now her expression was gloating. 'All men are heels, Ros,' she purred in a voice as smooth as cream.

'Some women are cats,' Ros retorted angrily.

They had professed to be friends—so much for friendship! She wouldn't have sneaked behind Glenis's back to make up to one of her boyfriends, and there were so many of them that one wouldn't have been missed. She was never short of somewhere to go or an escort to take her. She had more men dancing attendance on her at any one time than there were days in the week, yet she hadn't been able to keep her eyes off Ros's one and only.

Ros didn't doubt for a moment that Jarvis hadn't been more than willing, but she was certain that Glenis had started the flirting. She had been around long enough to see how

5

Glenis went to work on her victim of the moment. The pouting lower lip, the glance from under half-lowered lids, the straining buttons on her tight-fitting blouse and, should all else fail, the provocative way she had of sliding the palms of her hands over her thighs.

Whatever happened, irrespective of whether she patched it up with Jarvis, she was sure of one thing: she could no longer share a flat with Glenis. The moment she could make other arrangements for herself, she would pack her bags and go. Later, she was to wonder why her searching brain didn't stumble on the idea of taking up residence in Aunt Miranda's cottage immediately. There it was, with its repaired roof, new electrical wiring and up-to-date plumbing, just waiting for someone to occupy it, and hadn't the estate agent told her there would be little chance of attracting a buyer before spring? Apparently, rural cottages hadn't a lot to shout about until the first tender daffodil lifted its golden trumpet. But the cottage was over two hundred and fifty miles away, and her thoughts were contained nearer home, and so she didn't think about it straightaway. She couldn't seem to concentrate on anything beyond Jarvis's infidelity. It wasn't just the kiss, but to put it delicately, there had been a certain disarray about their persons that screamed at familiarity and told her she hadn't come upon a lone incident. It had been monstrous of them to carry on behind her back. Her anger was a constriction in her throat, an ache behind her eyes. As she lay down to sleep, bitter tears of disillusionment scorched her cheeks, scarring her belief in things she had taken for granted—codes of honor and common decency.

The idea of going to the cottage came to her on waking the next morning. There was no problem as far as her work was concerned. She had made a career for herself in cooking, writing about it and demonstrating it. She could work wherever there was a kitchen, and she was as portable as her typewriter. It struck her that there would be, in fact, a definite advantage in working in the solitude of the cottage, away from all distractions.

Pushing away her barely touched breakfast —her usual good appetite seemed to have deserted her—she went to phone her agent.

'Miles? Ros, here.' Without preliminaries she said, 'I'm going to Yorkshire, to the cottage.'

'That was a sudden decision! When do you intend to go? And for how long?'

'First thing tomorrow morning.' That would give her time to pack and tie up any loose ends. 'And for an indefinite period.'

'But it's winter.'

'Yes,' Ros said, looking out the window at a gray, fog-fretted world. 'That hasn't escaped my notice. Is it relevant?'

'It will be colder up north. You might even

7

be snowed in.'

'So?'

'I was thinking about your commitments.'

'I haven't forgotten. I've got the last recording to do for the television series.'

'And before that you've got a book-signing session.'

'Yes, on New Year's Day. I'll get back for those.'

'What if you can't? What if you really do get snowed in?'

Miles was a dear, but he did tend to fuss. 'You'll have to bring a big shovel and dig me out,' she scoffed gently. 'I know you seem to have gotten it into your head that it's a scatterbrained notion, but think about it. Amid all that lovely peace and tranquillity, I'll be able to shoot ahead with my new book.'

'Sounds as if you've finally gotten Jarvis to have a re-think about keeping the cottage,' Miles said on a note of inquiry.

She didn't want to broadcast the broken engagement in case it wasn't permanent, but Miles was discreet.

'Not exactly. I'm having a re-think about Jarvis.'

'Is that so?' His interest sparkled life into his voice. 'I can't say I approve of your going all that way away, but the re-think—I approve of that. So I'm not going to say another word to dissuade you. Am I right in thinking that the cottage isn't connected by phone?'

'Aunt Miranda didn't believe in telephones.'

'That, I take it, is a negative reply. However, I'm firmly convinced that the magic of the telephone will have penetrated even the wilds of deepest Yorkshire, so even if I can't phone you, at least you can phone me.'

His caring was a comfort to Ros. Miles was a bachelor in his late thirties, and though Ros was fond of him, she had never thought of him in romantic terms. On the other hand, he was much too magnetic and vital to be seen as a father figure. In any case, she already had a perfectly good father. True, he had always tended to be an absentee one, never on hand when she needed his support. At that moment, she had no idea where he was. The world was his oyster, and he could be anywhere. But at the same time, no one could take his place.

'I care about you, Ros. I want to know that you're all right.'

'Thank you for your concern, Miles. I appreciate it. I'll keep in touch, I promise. I'll give you a ring from somewhere when I get there to let you know that I've arrived safely.'

'Do that. Drive carefully.'

'Will do. Give my love to Hannah.' Hannah was the sister who lived with Miles and acted as his housekeeper.

Ros spent the day packing and notifying anyone that she felt should be notified of her move north. Jarvis came round in the evening. Again, he tried to win her over, but she shook

9

her head and declared adamantly, 'No, I've made up my mind. I've got to get away for a while.'

'What a fool I've been,' he said.

'The fault is never all on one side, Jarvis.' Now that her first surge of anger had subsided, she could see the situation through fairer eyes. 'It will do us good to be apart for a while, give us the chance to reassess our feelings. You'll know whether or not you'll be satisfied with just me. And if I do decide to sell the cottage, after all, at least I'll have had the satisfaction of living there for a spell. That's something I've got to get out of my system.'

'I'll miss you,' he said broodingly.

Not a word to the effect of 'How will you cope on your own? Will you be lonely away from the life you know, cut off from all your friends?' Just that selfish—and was she standing back and taking her first detached view of him because she amended that in her mind to *typically* selfish 'I'll miss you.'

'Jarvis, if you meet someone else or even decide that Glenis is the one for you, remember that you are now a free agent. But you must understand that the same counts for me. I also will regard myself as being without ties.'

Poor Jarvis, even though he was out of favor, she felt sorry for him. She realized that he expected his woman to meet certain requirements and that, in terms of these, she had quite a lot going for her. More than any man she knew, he appreciated good food, and as cooks go, she was considered to be among the best. He thought a woman should be decorative. And even while making the most cruelly candid assessment of her overall looks, which were admittedly not in Glenis's league of beauty, she couldn't deny that she had her good points. Her hair had the sheen of copper, with leaping red fires in its silky depths. Her gray eyes had chameleon qualities. In certain lights or in anger, they turned green. Her nose was neat—someone had once described it as deliciously pert; her mouth was full and warm, giving more than a hint of her true nature. Despite the fact that she was a trained cook who tucked in generously to the products of her profession, her figure was, although femininely curved, as lithesome and trim as if she starved on lettuce leaves. Even the restraint that Jarvis deplored in her manner had its nicer side. If she was sometimes less warm with him than he would have liked, he made no bones of the fact that her coolness to other men met with his wholehearted approval.

Jarvis was not showing approval now. On the contrary, he was looking most displeased. Now that her anger was on the wane, his was smoldering to the surface.

His handsome brow was tight as he said, 'Hasn't it occurred to you that my letting you

11

catch me like that might have been a Freudian slip? Good grief, Glenis isn't the first woman I've looked at since we got serious. But last night's blowup was the first spark of jealousy you've shown. It could be that I was beginning to think you didn't care. If nothing else, it's proved one thing to me, that you do.'

But did she? Wasn't that the whole crux of the matter, what she was really going away to find out? Had it been jealousy, or had she perhaps felt something else? Had she felt that she was being laughed at behind her back? Had she also objected to being made a fool of? If she'd been jealous, could she drag herself all those miles away from him, leaving him open to temptation? Jarvis was an extremely good-looking man. Blond hair, clean, wholesome, with perfect features, all the things that added up to give him bags of appeal to a woman. Miles said it was effeminate to be that perfect and that a lopsided nose, a chipped tooth or a crooked eyebrow would have given him some character. Miles said he was as bland as milk chocolate, but in fairness Miles didn't like Jarvis, and so his opinion didn't count. It was mutual—neither did Jarvis like Miles. Jarvis's connection with publishing meant he moved in Miles's circle, and of necessity they tolerated each other. That had always been a slight disappointment to Ros, who had wanted two men who figured so prominently in her life to like one another.

Next day, she said good-bye to Glenis. The flat had come fully furnished, so she didn't have the problem of disposing of unwanted pieces of furniture. Her rent was paid until the end of the month, which would give Glenis time to find another roommate to share the expenses with. Just before she closed the flat door for the last time, her eye fell on the calendar. It was the thirteenth. She hoped that wasn't a bad omen.

Until then, events, assisted by her own impulsive nature, had swept her along at such a pace that she'd hardly had time to draw breath, let alone think. The time to think was granted to her on the long journey north.

As she traveled, she thought about the events of the past few days. Had she been foolish to cut and run? Jarvis thought she was acting out of pique. But Miles understood. Bless him, he always did. She felt slightly dismayed at what she'd done, but excited. If it were wrong, how could it feel so right? She knew that it would seem strange living on her own again after sharing all that time. Despite her differences with Glenis, she would miss her. And—no disputing the fact—Hawthorn Cottage wouldn't be the same without Aunt Miranda. Great-aunt Miranda, really. The apple-cheeked old lady with the permanent grin had been her mother's aunt. She had taken Ros into her home and done her best to fill her mother's place after she had died. The

13

loss had been all the greater for the bewildered little girl because of her footloose father, whose job in civil engineering sent him careering round the world. Ros had wanted to make her home with her father, but Aunt Miranda had vetoed the idea. Explaining to Ros, she had said, 'Your father isn't a bad man, but I wouldn't wish to inflict his morals on an impressionable child.' Ros had expected her father to defend himself while at the same time putting up a fight to keep her with him. Instead, he had looked slightly relieved as he'd said, 'Aunt Miranda is right, Rusty. I would be a bad influence on you.'

Rusty was the name of her childhood—for the color of her hair. Now she was Ros, short for her given name of Rosalynd.

In spite of that nostalgic turn of thought, she did not travel unhappily, but drove for the most part on the tide of her growing enthusiasm, gaining greater certainty with every mile that swept under the hood of her car that she was doing the right thing.

The farmsteads and trees began to look like stenciled cutouts as she, and darkness, approached the village of Gillybeck. Of compact proportions, it had an endearing and friendly quaintness about it, with its cobbled square where market stalls were set up on Saturdays and Wednesdays and queer-shaped cottages lurked in unlikely corners.

She pulled up at the public telephone box to

honor her promise to Miles, sorted out a collection of the necessary coins and dialed his number.

On hearing the friendly and comforting familiarity of his voice, she said, 'I've arrived without mishap, and I'm in fine spirits, so you don't have to worry about me.'

'I was hoping you'd remember to ring. As it happens, I've had a phone call from your father.'

The line was atrocious. For a moment, she thought he'd said her father.

'Who did you say?'

'Your father,' he said.

Gracious he had!

'Obviously, he was trying to get in touch with you,' he went on. 'Glenis gave him my number, and he got through to me.'

'What did he want?'

The anxiety in her voice prompted Miles to say, 'No cause for alarm. Sorry, I should have put your mind at rest about his well-being straightaway.'

'Where was he phoning from?' Her father was grossly extravagant, finding it easier to pick up a phone rather than a pen, and it could have been from anywhere in the world.

She thought Miles said Australia, but there was another burst of static on the line, and so she couldn't be sure. It cleared, and she heard him say quite distinctly, 'He's been working with a guy who has returned to the U.K.

15

because of illness . . .' The line faded, and then she heard, '. . . said he'd look you up if he got the chance.'

'What did you say his name was, Miles?'

'Sorry, what's that? Can you shout up?'

She was shouting up.

'Is that better?'

'Better did you say? Not much.' He said something else that Ros couldn't catch. The static was now so bad that Ros only managed to get occasional snatches. '. . . nothing definite . . . might not show up . . . thought you should be warned just in case.' Warned about what?

Ros asked Miles to repeat what he'd said but gave up on realizing the hopelessness of it. Letting it go, she merely said, 'I'll look forward to seeing him, whoever he is.' Soon after that, she rang off.

On stepping out of the phone box, Ros decided not to return immediately to the car. After being confined behind the wheel for so long, she needed to stretch her legs. It was cold, yes, but she had anticipated that it would be, and so she'd layered herself with extra woollies accordingly. In any case, it was a crisp, invigorating coldness, and the air was like wine as she breathed it into her lungs.

By this time, the shops were closed and shuttered for the night. She had foolishly not stopped on the way to buy provisions, so unless she found somewhere to eat, she would go to

16

bed hungry. With that thought came the realization of just how hungry she was. Like the shops, the main street's cafés that catered to the daytime tourists were also closed. She knew she would be able to get a meal at the Gillybeck Arms, which served as both residential hotel and local pub, so she made her way there.

Later, she had no doubt, trade would pick up in the hotel's dining room, for the town wasn't noted for its variety of choice; but this early in the evening, she had the restaurant practically to herself. The exception was a family group enjoying high tea. The dinner menu wasn't supposed to be served until seven o'clock, and so certain things weren't available, but the obliging waitress said she thought the kitchen staff could come up with a grilled T-bone steak, and of course the dessert trolley was available, so Ros was well pleased.

She didn't hurry over her meal. It was pleasant to relax in that warm and comfortable atmosphere, and she was still there when the first of the early diners began to trickle in. Mostly twosomes and foursomes, but there was one man on his own.

She had put her cumbersome handbag on the floor by her chair, and he kicked it as he passed. They both apologized at once, she for leaving it at such a careless angle, he for kicking it.

He bent to retrieve it, examining it for

damage as his long, lean frame uncoiled with the grace of an animal. His hair was thick and smooth, the color of ebony. His face was deeply tanned; he was either a sun worshipper, or he worked long hours out-of-doors in a country where the sun was much fiercer than here. His features were strong—harsh was the word that flung itself into her mind. It was the type of face that Miles would have said was full of character, lopsided nose and all. Had he been born with that tilt to one side of his nose or gained it in a punch-up? He had the kind of broad shoulders that suggested he would be handy with his fists. In contrast to the satanic hard lines of his face, his mouth came as a shock. It was too full, hinting at an inner sensuality. His eyes complemented his mouth —dark brown, the color of woodsmoke, emitting more sex appeal than any one man should be allowed to pack. They lifted from inspecting her handbag for any outward sign of the abuse it had just received, and as they played over her face, her knees turned to jelly. She had an uncanny sensation of déjà vu. Someone, somewhere in her past, had created feelings similar to these, if not quite taking the same form.

He clearly registered her reaction; indeed, the glazing of contempt that came to his eyes told her that it was one he was used to and found boring.

'It doesn't seem to have come to any harm,'

he said, and even though the scorn that was so apparent in his eyes had now slid into his voice, the deep and slightly husky tone was still attractive.

She swallowed, hating herself for responding to his masculinity and hating him for knowing that she found him so disturbingly interesting.

'Thank you,' she said.

In accepting her handbag, her fingers brushed with his. She jerked back as if a naked flame had touched her, and that was just what the sensation had been like.

She expected him to depart then, but he did not. Instead of continuing on his way, he remained where he was and surveyed her for a moment. The woodsmoke eyes no longer contained that gleam of derision but smoldered in speculation. The nature of that speculation was unknown to her; that it wasn't to his liking was obvious in the grim frown that touched his lips. She couldn't be sure, but she felt that his awesome self-assurance had slipped a little.

From her own point of view, she was overwhelmingly conscious of two things: her quickened pulse beat and her crumpled appearance. He was the most maddeningly handsome man she had ever come across, and it had to be when she was feeling considerably less than her best, after a long and tiring day's drive. She had gone into the ladies' room before coming into the restaurant, but only to

19

pay court to hygiene and wash the grime from her fingers. She hadn't bothered to comb her hair or touch up her makeup, and her comfortable traveling gear—trousers and thick-knit sweater—were hardly Bond Street. In contrast to his clothes, they didn't seem all that far removed from the rags category. He was superbly turned out in tasteful country tweeds. She knew how poor Cinders felt—but her prince was blocking her exit, and she could hardly push him out of the way to make her escape.

Collecting up her coat from where she had deposited it on the spare chair, she said, 'Excuse me, please,' and rose to her feet with dignity.

'Certainly,' he said, looking momentarily puzzled, as though wondering what he was still doing there as he moved aside to let her pass.

She felt his eyes boring into the back of her as she walked away. Even though it made her feel uneasy, she was flattered by his attention. She lifted her head, walking tall and trying to swing freely from the hips with jaunty nonchalance, just as if devastating men were in the habit of following her with their eyes. Actually, her figure adapted well to trousers, and she had quite a neat rear view; not that it would be apparent now that she was snuggled in her bulky sheepskin coat.

She sailed out of the swinging door. Only then could she relax. No, she couldn't. She heard his step pounding after her. That was unbelievable. To be looked at was one thing, but to be chased after—wow! She might not have had Cinderella's fairy godmother on hand to deck her out in the kind of impression-making clothes she would have liked him to see her in, but she must have done something right.

Wrong again. In her confusion, she had only walked out without paying her bill—and it was with that transgression that he was about to confront her. Not that she knew it straightaway, but when the realization was bluntly driven home to her, it made her feel even more of a fool.

His mantle of self-assurance was firmly back in place as he trapped her wrist in a blood-stopping grip and inquired in the most sardonic drawl she had ever heard, 'Haven't you forgotten something?'

Still it didn't click. She checked. Handbag, gloves, scarf. 'No, I appear to have everything, thank you.'

'Enjoy your meal, did you?'

'Yes, it was very—oh, my goodness!' At last, it dawned on her. In the kind of 'pale' voice that went with vividly flushed cheeks, she choked out in alarm, 'I walked out without paying.'

'Precisely. It's a quaint British custom that unfortunately must be observed.'

'You don't think I did it on purpose, do

you?'

'Oh, no, I wouldn't think anything of the sort,' he said in a tone that hinted at just the reverse. 'I'm quite sure it was an oversight.'

'It was.' How dare he be so insulting! Damn his mocking, arrogant smile. That smile? It teased the edge of her awareness. She was more certain than ever that she knew him from somewhere. It rankled that she couldn't remember where. 'And even if it wasn't, what's it got to do with you?'

'Nothing. I'm just a public-minded citizen doing my duty.'

He soon made it known to her what he considered that duty to be—to accompany her as she suffered the ignominy of having to go back inside and rectify her shameful omission. And did he have to keep such a tight hold of her wrist? She was returning voluntarily. She didn't need the assistance of a jailer. Yet even in her temper, she registered the thought that it was a nice hand, large and strong, dependable. The kind of hand you'd want on your side in times of trouble.

Attempting to thrust it off, she said, 'Do you mind! I'm not about to run away.'

That secured her release and allowed her to skip a pace ahead of him.

The waitress looked coyly amused and brushed aside Ros's apology, saying, 'Please don't give it another thought. It's easy to tell that you usually have an escort to pay for you.'

The girl meant to be kind and said that to put Ros at her ease; but her awareness of his wry nod of agreement added to her frustration. In these days of equal pay, she did not go through life sponging off men but accepted the sharing of expenses as the fair price to pay for women's much-prized equality. She knew that not all women thought this way; some chose to accept the liberation but shun the liability. Glenis, for example, brought her own logic to bear on the subject and never paid even when her man friend earned less than she did. She justified that by saying that women's expenses were higher and she needed her money to buy the pricey cosmetics and clothes to make herself lovelier for her male escort. She said that men liked to be seen with a well-dressed, expensively turned out woman, and therefore they should pay for the privilege.

Ros settled the offending bill. Then, angered by his mocking assumption that she was the same as those women, she added a monstrously generous tip, to make up, and left.

This time no pounding steps followed her. She didn't know what she was getting into a state about. It didn't matter what he thought of her. Probably she would never see him again. That would suit her perfectly well. He could only serve as an added complication in a life that was complicated enough already.

# CHAPTER TWO

It was quite dark. Trees met overhead, turning the road into a black canyon. The car's headlights picked up ghostly shapes. A small animal darted into their beams before scurrying away to safety.

Ros thought about the haven of Aunt Miranda's old-fashioned high bed, as soft as thistledown. As a child, she had found it difficult to climb into and had used a small stool to give her a leg up and then dived into its enfolding softness. Her child's vivid imagination had conjured up stories around the patchwork quilt, making mountains out of her knees that the handsome prince then charged up on his pure white steed to rescue the fair maiden held captive in pillow castle.

She thought her imagination wouldn't have much leeway that night. She was so achingly tired she knew that she would fall asleep instantly.

After going on seemingly forever and forging deeper and deeper into isolation, she finally slowed down to negotiate the turnoff road that led to Hawthorn Cottage. The potholed road was hazardous even in daytime. It served only two cottages. Hawthorn Cottage forked off to the left, Holly Cottage to the right. So she supposed the authorities didn't think it merited the cost of keeping it in good repair. She wondered if Mrs. Heath still lived at Holly Cottage. If her memory served her correctly, she was younger than Aunt Miranda. The two cottages, both named after prickly shrubs with red berries, had always caused a certain amount of confusion. Inevitably, Ros had frequently acted as delivery girl, taking parcels and letters to Mrs. Heath that had gotten to Hawthorn Cottage in error. At first, Ros had gone to Mrs. Heath's in fear and trepidation, but a rewarding wedge of homemade pie or oven cake, the latter split and buttered while warm so that the butter melted into the fragrant fluffy softness of the inside, had gone a long way to soothing her qualms, and she had begun to look for excuses to visit. Ros had quickly come to realize that Mrs. Heath had a lot in common with her oven cake. She was only crusty on the outside.

On losing her initial shyness, she had accepted Mrs. Heath's invitation to visit anytime, and an unlikely friendship had developed between the taciturn old lady and the introverted young girl. Sometimes, when visitors had overflowed at Hawthorn Cottage, she had slept in the tiny spare room at Holly Cottage. The only time she hadn't liked going there had been when Mrs. Heath's grandson was staying with her. He had been a gypsy-dark youth back then, ten years her senior; so that by the time she had reached the age of ten, he had been double her age, a man. Everyone had said then he was good-looking, but in Ros's eyes he had appeared sinister. In all the stories she'd read, the good prince had been golden-haired, while the black-haired prince had been the wicked villain to be feared—as she had feared him. His name was Cliff Heath. She had taken one look at that saturnine face and had naturally called him Heathcliff.

Mrs. Heath had fallen about laughing when she had first heard Ros address him by this name, but not so her grandson. He had looked fiercer than ever and made as though to pounce on Ros, causing her to tremble in her shoes and regret her boldness. Mrs. Heath had insisted that he was only teasing, but Ros hadn't been so sure. Usually, she had believed implicitly in Mrs. Heath's wisdom, but this had been one time when she had felt more inclined to trust the evidence of her own eyes, and a stolen, under-her-lashes glance had seen all that forbidding black disapproval.

She had been twelve at the most when, to her immense relief, he'd gone to work abroad. He had been in the same line as her father— civil engineering. She had always believed that his admiration of her father had influenced his choice. She wondered as she approached the cottages what Heathcliff had made of his life and where he was. She remembered her father's once saying that he was brave and

26

reckless and brilliant, that he had the ability to be anything he chose and would go far. She hadn't thought of him in years. She wondered what perverse twist of fate had made her think of him then and realized with a start of surprise that she had seen a fleeting resemblance to him in the man who had magnetized her thoughts in the Gillybeck Arms. *He* couldn't possibly have been Heathcliff— could he? No, she'd known an instant aversion to Heathcliff, keen enough to last a lifetime and totally at variance with the feelings that the stranger had aroused in her.

She brought the car to a somewhat jerky and grinding halt outside Hawthorn Cottage— which arrival, even with due consideration to the appalling condition of the road, was far removed from her usual proficient driving standard. Her concentration was elsewhere.

She was surprised to observe that the old gate was still tied up with a piece of wire, just as it had been the last time she had been there. That was odd. The same old gate, in the same state of disrepair. She remembered no mention of a new gate on the sheaf of invoices she had received, yet she would have thought that a new gate would have had some priority in the repairs. If that was a small matter of disconcertion, her next finding came as a shock. Her key, the brand-new key that had been mailed to her to fit the newly fixed locks, wouldn't fit. That was very strange indeed.

She stumbled back down the overgrown, uneven flags of the path to her car and rummaged in the glove compartment for her flashlight. Playing the beam over the cottage, she saw that the roof, the windows, everything, were in the same state of disrepair as she had last seen, when she came to inspect her inheritance.

She got back into her car, huddled forlornly behind the steering wheel and shivered, mainly from the cold cut of the wind blowing down from the moor but also from a tiny sliver of alarm. What did it mean? And where did she go from here? She had thrown her old key away, and she didn't feel like breaking her way in. In any case, what would be the point? The cottage wouldn't be habitable. The gate hadn't been replaced, the roof still had a whopping great hole in it, and it would be a fair guess that the inside repairs hadn't been carried out, either. Tomorrow she'd make an early call on the agent in charge of the work and find out what was going on, but where did that leave her tonight? Right out in the cold. She could, she supposed, go back to Gillybeck and book a room for the night at the Gillybeck Arms, but it was a long way; she had been driving all day, and she was exhausted.

The next idea that came into her mind was infinitely more appealing. Why didn't she do what she used to do when her gregarious aunt had filled the cottage with people to bursting point, that is, beg a bed for the night at Holly Cottage? That would only entail going partway down the dark and treacherous road and taking the other fork. She had called at Holly Cottage the last time she was there, but no one had been at home. In the old days, it had been Mrs. Heath's habit to trek across the moor to the farm in the next hollow to buy dairy produce, so that's where she could have been. On the other hand, it was possible that she felt too old to be living in such an isolated spot on her own and had found accommodation elsewhere. The thought skipped across her mind that she remembered hearing Mrs. Heath say that if ever Aunt Miranda left, she would make a home for herself with one of her children. She had just one daughter; Ros recalled that her name was Alice. And one son, Howard, who was Heathcliff's father.

In a matter of minutes, she brought the car to a stop outside Holly Cottage. It was in darkness, but that told Ros very little, because old ladies tended to go to bed early.

Ros opened the gate, noticing how easily it swung back on its hinges, and, without hazard, walked up the evenly flagged path. M'm— strange. The door, like the gate, was also new. The last time she had been there, the cottage hadn't been in a much better state than Aunt Miranda's. Obviously, Mrs. Heath had set her home in order. Or someone had.

If Mrs. Heath still lived there, would it be an

29

imposition to knock on her door? A voice in her head seemed to say, 'Certainly not, girl. Don't be fainthearted. Get on with it.'

Upon that, Ros raised her hand to the door knocker, bringing it down three times. If Mrs. Heath had sold out and she found that she had roused a stranger from his or her bed, surely, in the circumstances, her explanation and apology would gain sympathy, and then she could follow her first idea and try her luck at the Gillybeck Arms.

Although she knocked again, still no one answered, and a thread of suspicion, already alerted, began to weave itself deeper into her thoughts. She remembered all those instances in the past when the two cottages had been confused, when someone had taken the left fork instead of the right, or vice versa. Mistakes were made. Only last week she read an account in the newspaper of the wrong building's being demolished. She had a sheaf of invoices in her possession to prove that repairs had been carried out somewhere. Not at Hawthorn Cottage, to be certain. So . . .

There was one sure-fire way to find out. She took from her pocket the key that the agent had sent to her. If that fitted the lock, there would be little doubt in her mind that the repairs she had paid for had been carried out at Holly Cottage by mistake.

The key slid in effortlessly and turned with the same ease. Ros located the light switch without difficulty. She entered, not without a certain amount of trepidation. She supposed the ethics of the situation would still amount to trespass, but no way could she not have gone in and looked round. It was a tremendous relief to see Mrs. Heath's homely furniture in the newly decorated rooms even though, when she ventured upstairs, her tentative peep into the master bedroom brought no trace of her old and very dear friend.

That brought a sigh of gentle regret to her mouth. She felt frustrated and perplexed.

Tomorrow, someone would have some explaining to do. As far as tonight was concerned, she knew what she was going to do. She was going to sleep in the spare room at the end of the passage, the one she'd always been given in the old days. In her child's imagination, the strip of corridor had been the drawbridge leading to her own private domain. How could that be trespassing?

Feeling better, she trotted back down to the car and took out the suitcase that contained the necessities for an overnight stay, leaving the rest of her things where they were. She took the trouble to lock the car out of city precaution. Silly, because there was no likelihood of anyone's taking anything out there in this remote place.

Her night-time preparations were less meticulous than usual. She washed her face sparingly "round the moon,' as Aunt Miranda used to say, skimping on ears and neck, and her teeth were accordingly brushed in a hand count of seconds. She promised her ears, neck and teeth a more thorough clean in the morning. It was out of character for her to be slatternly like that, but she was too dropping tired to be anything else. She pulled her nightgown over her head, removing the pins from her hair, which billowed out and then ran down her back like a shimmering flame. She picked up her hairbrush, applied a few indifferent strokes, abandoning the effort at the fast tangle, and then reveled in the ultimate joy of sinking into bed and closing her eyes. Her last drowsy thoughts concerned the fact that the bed was made up, as if in expectation of her coming. Surely that must be a good omen?

Her long and peaceful night's sleep was not to be. She woke with a start to hear someone moving about downstairs. Her first disoriented thought was that she was back in the flat she had shared with Glenis and the tenant who had the flat below was making more noise than usual.

The realization of where she was gave her heart a guilty jolt. The footsteps were now coming up the stairs. She sat up in bed, hugging her knees and trying to decide what to do. She didn't feel menaced, even though she knew the tread was too heavy to belong to

Mrs. Heath. The thought that it might be a burglar never entered her sleep-bemused mind. Burglars had richer pickings in mind and wouldn't waste time on an apparently humble cottage.

No, obviously someone other than Mrs. Heath lived there. The question was should she make her presence known or hope that he—because those footsteps were definitely male—went into his own bedroom? In which case, two more alternatives would be facing her. She could wait until he'd fallen asleep and then creep out and make her escape. Or she could do what she had planned to do: spend the night where she was and face the consequences in the morning.

Even as her bedroom door was flung open so savagely that it crashed back on its hinges, she saw the flaw in her reasoning. He would have seen the car parked outside and knew that he had a squatter.

The voice, one that was painfully familiar to her since she had heard it so recently, shot out at her in the darkness. 'All right, I'm going to put the light on. In case you're about to try anything foolish, it's only fair to warn you that I'm a judo black belt.'

The light went on one second before Ros had the presence of mind to draw the bedclothes up to her chin. And then it was too late, and the opportunity was lost to her. Her wrists were clamped in a viciously cruel hold,

33

she was flung back down on the bed, and her arms were propelled swiftly above her head; simultaneously, the springs creaked under his additional weight.

In petrified, horrified dismay, she stared into woodsmoke eyes that held on to their fierceness for a moment, positively glinting with murderous intent, then smoldered with amusement as he ejaculated, 'What the hell! If it isn't Rusty again.'

His use of that childhood pet name, the name her father still called her by, told all.

'Heathcliff,' she said weakly.

He frowned, just as he had used to in the old days, as he corrected, 'Cliff. Did you know who I was back at the Arms?'

'No. Your face was familiar, somehow, so I thought you must be a lookalike of someone I knew. The suspicion came later who you might be. The fact that you're here, in your grandmother's cottage, proves conclusively that you are. Did you know me? I mean before you came upon me now?'

'No. Like you, I was puzzled. I thought you reminded me of someone. I expect I would have gotten it eventually. You must have been about eleven or twelve when I last saw you. A skinny little thing with carroty pigtails. Since then, you've—er—done some growing up.'

He hadn't let go of her wrists, and her arms in their captive position above her head made the modest covering of her brushed nylon

34

nightgown strain immodestly across her breasts. His eyes made a deliberate play upon the points that more visually differentiate between child and woman. His lusty, tormenting attention burgeoned her nipples to such an extent that the twin buds seemed about to prod through the material. He would know by that fact alone that the pulses pounding beneath his powerful fingers were beating out—more than anger or fear—her shameful awareness of his masculinity.

Before bounding in on her, he had removed his jacket and tie, she supposed so that he would be less hampered if he was called upon to use brute strength to evict the intruder. She was conscious of the powerful muscles rippling across his chest and down his arms, the warmth and desirability that radiated from him as he remained poised above her. His nearness bothered her; the intimacy of lying on the same bed with a man who was so overwhelmingly male was too much to take. Her eyes drifted up to his face, surmounting each obstacle that seemed hellbent on seducing her senses, the solid strength of his chin, the sensuality of his mouth, the lopsided nose that hadn't been that way the last time they met, finally coming to rest upon the most dangerous feature of all, those soul-burning eyes. Eyes that were capable of enticing a girl beyond the bounds of common sense into self-destructive madness.

In the old days, she had always skirted

round him with extreme caution, sensing that he was someone to be feared. She couldn't have known that that was only the tip of the iceberg and that the danger about him would have these whirlpool depths. She knew it wasn't the fierceness of his grip that was stopping her circulation but the pounding fury of her own blood that threatened to block her arteries.

'As fascinating as it is to share a bed with you, do you mind removing yourself? You're hurting my wrists.'

The words were fine, as flippant as she would have wished; it was the delivery of them that was all wrong. She hadn't reckoned with the lack of control she would have over her voice. The husky drawl that emerged did not have the intended mocking impact and was received with sardonic amusement, even though that did accompany the release of her wrists.

'I'm sorry,' he said, swinging away from her, rolling over on his hip and standing up. 'That's the first time I've ever apologized for sharing a lady's bed.'

Only pausing long enough to pull the bedclothes up to her chin, she said, 'I can imagine.'

'You always did have a vivid imagination,' he replied, the smile that hovered on his mouth increasing and with it her consternation at her own gaucherie. Because she had asked

36

for that.

'Explanation time, do you think?' he said. 'There must be a reason other than the strange attraction that flared between us back at the Gillybeck Arms. I don't usually score this early. Or did I—' His head went to one side. 'And has the lady had a change of heart?'

'Of course not. I'm not the least bit attracted to you,' she lied valiantly. 'I hated you as a child, and our meeting up again hasn't caused me to revise my opinion. You used to frighten me deliberately, and that hasn't altered. You're still doing it. You are even more obnoxious than I remembered.'

'You reckon? Obnoxious enough to turn you out into the bleak, cold night?'

She bit on her lip. He wouldn't—would he? He wouldn't turn her out, but he could make it pretty uncomfortable for her. It might be in her own best interest to back down gracefully, hateful as that idea was, before he forced her to.

'Not that obnoxious,' she retracted with more discretion than liking.

'Would you like some hot chocolate?' he asked. At her startled glance, he added, 'I've an idea that it's going to be a long and involved tale. That being so, it might be as well to prime the pump.'

'In that case, yes, please, if you're having some.' She giggled despite herself.

'What's so funny?'

37

'The absurdity of being offered something as homely as hot chocolate by a man who has just grabbed me with murderous designs on my body.'

'Ah . . . but the designs were only murderous to begin with. They changed quite rapidly when, instead of the husky male I expected to tackle, I found myself in combat with a delectable female in my bed, dressed in—or should I say?—in a state of undress.'

'You're doing it again.'

'What?'

'Frightening me.'

'Am I?'

'No. But only because I'm not easily frightened. I'm warning you, I will not tolerate this—this persecution.'

'No?'

The one-word taunt made its mark on a temper that was too easily provoked, and her mouth compressed itself around an equally challenging 'No!'

He leaned over, moving in close enough for his breath to fan her temple and for her to be enveloped in the sensuous net of his expensive aftershave. Neither was it just the way he smelled, but also the way he looked at her under sliding lids in a manner that was most damaging to her good intentions, which were not to let him goad her into flaring up at him in antagonism. And, conversely, to keep feeling antagonistic toward him, having decided that

that was less dangerous than allowing herself to respond to his compelling male attraction. How could anyone so polished in satire and derision flaunt his masculinity in a way that was earthy in its primitiveness? Even though there was ice in his clipped one-word taunt, he had started a fire in her veins. It didn't help to cool the active cauldron of her emotions to see the glint of intelligence in his eyes that told her that he was aware of the this-way-that-way tug of her impassioned, overzealous thoughts.

He placed a kiss on the tip of his finger and transferred it to her mouth. It was a feather-light touch that had the impact of a rain of hailstones and raised goose bumps all over her skin. The satisfaction of jerking her head back in rejection was denied her by the withdrawal of the finger, which was removed as swiftly as it had come.

'I won't be long,' he said.

Ros couldn't make out the intonation. Threat or promise? She had no intention of waiting to find out. She couldn't think of anything more beset with hazards than having him sit on the edge of the bed, with her explaining her presence in it over a cozy cup of hot chocolate. At least she had a sporting chance of keeping her equilibrium intact with the kitchen table between them.

The moment he went through the door, she got up, pulled on her warm plaid dressing gown and unconsciously followed the natural feminine instinct of brushing her hair. When she realized what that gesture implied, namely, that she was making sure her appearance was pleasing to his eye, she jerked her hair back in her fingers so angrily that her scalp tingled in painful protest. She confined the silken red cloud into a tight coil at the nape of her neck, knowing that she would be grateful for the extra composure the severity of that style would give her. Long hair seemed to have a sensuous appeal; the color of hers was noted for firing a man's imagination. As she followed Heathcliff down the stairs, she lamented silently to herself that she could do little about its vibrant color. It was a lament not often made these days. As a child, she had hated its color, but the years had had a pleasant mellowing effect on it that in no way detracted from its richness, and she had come to recognize it as an asset. In this instance, however, it was one asset she could do without; it might even be regarded as a liability.

He was heating milk at the stove. His eyes acknowledged her presence and then marked her progress as she crossed the kitchen and pulled a stool up to the table. From this perch, she meditated further on her position. She couldn't see him being gallant enough to take himself off to the Gillybeck Arms for the night, and as she had already decided that she didn't fancy venturing out, she could surmise that they would be spending the night under the same roof. That being so, she would be prudent if she behaved with natural coolness and decorum and ignored totally his shameless baiting. She didn't really believe that he was drawn to her in that way. There was something too calculating about his manner; it was cold, mockery based. The methods he'd used to frighten her as a child would have no impact anymore, so he had resorted to other tactics to fit the updated situation. It was difficult to assess, and she could be wrong, but she didn't think he was flirting with her for the usual reasons of attraction but rather because of his perverse streak—that she had first perceived in him all those years ago—that delighted in tormenting her. She realized that it would be to her advantage, if she could manage it, to treat him as an annoying figure of her past whom she'd had the misfortune to meet up with again. At the same time, because of the vulnerability of her position and because of her wish not to be turned out at this unearthly hour, a certain amount of diplomacy would be advisable.

A foaming mug of hot chocolate was placed before her.

'That was some sigh,' he observed.

'I was wondering how to begin explaining,' she admitted, not untruthfully. 'An appalling mistake has been made—at least I think it has. Unless you or your grandmother authorized

41

the modernizations that have been carried out here, by any chance?'

His eyes glanced over the streamlined, modern kitchen with its practical wall units and appliances. 'No, neither of us did,' he said. 'I'm managing my grandmother's affairs for her. At her time of life, she can do without the hassle. When I let myself in yesterday, it came as a huge surprise to find the reverse of what I expected. Instead of looking forlorn and broken down, everything was in immaculate order.'

'The locks have been changed. It would be interesting to know how you did get in.'

'A bit of expertise, on a back window. Not too difficult when you know how.'

'Remind me to put the family jewels in the vault at the bank when you are in the vicinity,' she joked. 'I'm happy to know that your grandmother is still alive, and well, I hope?'

'Considering her age, she is in remarkably good health. And just as salty as she always was.'

Ros chuckled. 'I'm delighted to hear it. Couldn't imagine her any other way.'

'Spare a thought for my poor Aunt Alice, who has to bear the brunt of her querulous tongue.'

'Sorry, Aunt Alice,' Ros said, still smiling. 'I didn't mean it exactly that way. So your grandmother is living with her daughter. I had wondered if she might be.'

'She packed up and left here when your aunt died. She said it was too lonely without her. I'm sorry about that, Rusty. I know how close you were. You had a unique aunt-niece relationship.'

Ros's lower lip trembled. She still hadn't got over the loss of her Aunt Miranda, and neither was she as immune as she would have wished to his unexpected kindness and understanding. 'I just wish I'd appreciated her more. I took her for granted.'

Her mug was removed from her fingers and returned to the table. He took both her hands in his and looked deep into her eyes. Her view of him was just a bit blurred because of the shimmer in her eyes.

'Love is taking someone for granted. It's knowing without being told. The words are just the frosting on the cake. Tell me, Rusty, since you heard about your aunt's death, have you, let your hair down and cried?'

'Yes.'

'I don't mean a few polite, stiff-upper-lip tears. Have you let it all come out and had a real good howl? M'mmm? You should, you know. It would do you a world of good.'

He let go of one of her hands, and his fingers stroked her cheek before moving round to where her hair nestled in its confined knot at the nape of her neck. 'Letting your hair down is good for you—in every way.' She hadn't realized what his intention was, so

43

deftly did he remove the pins holding it securely in place, until the richness of her hair was flowing over his hands. 'There, that's better. The schoolmarmish look isn't you at all.'

She couldn't explain it, but it was as if in taking the pins out he had released not only her hair but also the flood of emotions that had been contained in a hard shell of coldness inside her. He was right. When something as soul shattering as death hit you, why did you have to trap your feelings behind a brave smile? Because of her mother's early death and the fact that her father traveled extensively in the course of his work, she and her aunt had been close. Aunt Miranda had been everything to her.

'She did everything for me,' she sobbed. 'She bandaged my knees, clothed and cared for me and encouraged me to take up a career.'

She realized that she hadn't wanted to hang on to Hawthorn Cottage for its own sake. Jarvis had been right about the impracticality of keeping it. It was isolated, frequently cut off by huge snowdrifts for months in winter that all too often lasted for eight months of the year. The beauty of it in summer could not counteract the fact that it was too far away from the pulse point of their livelihoods. It didn't make any difference; she still wanted to keep it, if only for a while. Somehow that

44

would make it less of a betrayal when she did eventually part with it. When it hadn't sold, something in her had rejoiced. The idea of coming up there to work in glorious hibernation for the winter had appealed enormously. But everything had gone wrong. Because of someone's incompetence, the repairs had been carried out on the wrong cottage. She'd been cheated, because no way could she live at Hawthorn Cottage—work there and let time take away her grief at losing Aunt Miranda—in its present state.

'Come on, Rusty. Let go!' he commanded.

And suddenly she was in his arms and weeping wildly. Even when the shudders ceased, he still held her face pressed tightly to the solid bulk of his chest. It made her feel very safe, protected.

The hand that had been stroking her hair came round to tilt her chin.

'Better?'

'Mm,' she said, gazing up at him mistily. 'I needed that. I would never have suspected you of having such tender insight.'

One black eyebrow arched in cynicism. 'Nor have I, so don't go crediting me with finer feelings. The pigtailed child knew best. She recognized me for the deep-dyed villain that I am. Hold on to that impression, Rusty. It will save you a lot of disillusionment. Now, off to bed with you.'

'But I haven't explained why I'm here.'

'You don't need to. It doesn't require much brain searching to figure out what's happened. Somebody's bungled. The repair work has been carried out on the wrong cottage. I'm here by right of the fact that Holly Cottage belongs to my family. But the new chimney stack, the electrical wiring, a new damp course, the refitted kitchen—oh, and don't let's forget the decorations—are all yours. We'll work something out in the morning.'

'Right, then. I'll go to bed.'

'Yours is the big bedroom.'

'But I'm quite happy with the small room at the end of the passage.'

'That's up to you. I should point out, though, that I made the bed up for myself, and I don't intend to give it up, but—'

Without warning, he drew her forward again. His hands splayed themselves low across her back, bringing her hips up close to the muscled hardness of his thighs. Satan himself lurked in his smoldering eyes.

'You'll move out of that room for me?' She completed the sentence for him on a husky note of inquiry.

She should pull away. His hold was containing her lightly enough to make that possible, but she didn't seem able to instruct her legs to take the first positive step. A dark enchantment was enfolding her that she couldn't—or wouldn't, because she didn't want to—flee from.

'No, Rusty.'

'No?'

'I was going to say, if you're so minded, you're at liberty to share it with me. Of course, it's a comparatively small bed for a man of my build, so you may have to face the consequences. If I kick out, you won't have much room to squirm away.'

Even as she looked at him in horror, both repelled and fascinated by this unbelievable conversation, his jaw thrust out aggressively. 'I was only joking.' His frown deepened. 'There's something about you, always was even when you were a scrap of a child with huge condemning eyes, that provokes me to torment you.'

His hands dropped away, and he took the stride back that she should have taken, and this gave her free passage. The door, her escape route, was but a few shaky steps away. She looked back over her shoulder at him, but he was busying himself with rinsing out the mugs at the sink, and so his expression was denied her. Damn! She should have done that menial task. To be employed at something so everyday made him seem too human, and it suited her purpose to regard him as a monster.

'Good night, Rusty,' he said, not turning around but keeping his back to her, his voice a deep and commanding dismissal.

'Good night,' she said, and took the giddy swirl of her emotions up the stairs.

47

No way was she going to risk any more challenging involvement this night, and so she made her way to the master bedroom. The bed there wasn't made up, but she knew where the necessaries were kept and soon rectified that.

Surprisingly, in view of all that had happened, she fell almost instantly into a dreamless sleep.

## CHAPTER THREE

If she thought she was going to spend the remainder of the night undisturbed, she was in for a rude awakening. And that was exactly what she got.

A voice, or voices, roused her. She struggled up through the blanketing mists of sleep to the bemused awareness of an argument in progress. Sliding cautiously out of her bed, she tiptoed stealthily to the door, opening it a crack. No one was in the hallway at the top of the stairs, or the passage, for that matter. The talking had now stopped, and there was an uncanny quiet. She wondered if the voices had been in her own head. Had she been having one of those terribly realistic dreams that seem too true not to have happened?

Shrugging her shoulders, she was gently easing the door shut when the hysterical mumblings started up again. This time there was absolutely no doubt in her mind. This terrible discord of sound was coming from the small room at the end of the passage where Heathcliff was sleeping. Even though he had corrected her that his name was Cliff—he'd always hated being called Heathcliff—she thought that he would always be Heathcliff to her. She was racing down the passage in a flash; her hand was actually on the doorknob before a thought struck her that hastily jerked it back. What if her first assumption that he was ill was incorrect?

Just for supposition, what if he'd had someone with him when he had returned this evening, a lady friend who had waited in the car and had been let in when she went to bed? No. He wouldn't have resorted to secrecy. He would have brought his woman in openly. He was his own master and could bring home whom he liked. In any case, these weren't lovemaking moans. He wasn't groaning in pleasure but in distress.

This time her hand did not draw back from the doorknob, and within seconds her flying feet had taken her to his bed. He had drawn back the curtains before getting in, and the moon washed across the greenish-gray pallor of his face, highlighting the sharp angles of his cheekbones, which seemed to stretch his skin to an unbelievable tautness in an expression of acute agony. He was writhing and mumbling; perspiration stood out in beads on

49

his forehead. She didn't know what to do. A dreadful inadequacy held her captive that she had to struggle free of, and then she was racing all the way back down the passage to the bathroom, which was situated next to the master bedroom, for cloths and towels to sponge him down.

She realized how limited her knowledge of first-aid was and acted solely on impulse. His brow was on fire; his body was a burning furnace, yet his teeth were chattering, and he was shivering as though he were in the grip of freezing ice. As she sponged his face, she had to dodge his thrashing arms and legs. She wasn't too adept at getting out of the way, and he scored one rather nasty blow on the side of her face. She persevered regardless, murmuring words meant to soothe and comfort throughout her ministrations. Finally, he seemed to sink into an uneasy sleep.

All this time she hadn't had much opportunity to think what she should do next; she had been too busy doing it. But now indecision held her again. He really ought to be gotten out of those wet pajamas, and the sheets, which were also damp and clammy from his perspiration, should be changed. She had never seen a naked man before, but it wasn't squeamishness that prevented her from stripping him but lack of strength. She had a go at moving one arm, but it was a dead-weight, and she was defeated before she began.

She wondered if she ought to take her car and go into Gillybeck to rouse the doctor but decided against it. She hadn't been able to leave him before, and now that he seemed to be over the worst of whatever it was, she decided that it was pointless as well as cruelly inconsiderate to drag a busy, overworked practitioner from his much-needed sleep.

She still didn't feel that she could abandon him and go to her own room. He might wake up and wonder what had happened. She didn't want him to be confused or unduly worried. She found a pair of clean pajamas in one of the drawers in the chest of drawers and sorted out clean sheets from the linen cupboard in case he did wake up and she could manage to swap his pajamas and change the bed. Then she returned briefly to her own room for the quilt on her bed, and this she wrapped round herself. Then she curled up in the padded armchair to rest as best she could. Sleep was out of the question; she was much too agitated and concerned.

It was an uneasy vigil. Time crawled. It seemed like an hour, although it could only have been ten or so minutes before he opened his eyes.

'Rusty . . . what the blazes! Oh . . . obviously I woke you. I'm sorry. I . . . er . . . hope you weren't too alarmed.'

'If it's something you know about, you might

51

have warned me. You scared the life out of me,' she said, incensed by his apparently nonchalant attitude.

'Cool it, spitfire. I didn't think it was necessary. Just in case you had to go to the bathroom during the night, I made sure you had a room at that side of the house.'

'Oh! Was that why you acted like you did?'

'I thought I was far enough away from you for you not to hear anything in case I did have an attack. Perhaps I make more noise than I realized.'

'I'll vouch for that. Attack of what? I cursed not having a phone. I didn't know whether I should have gone for the doctor.'

'I'd have skinned you alive if you had. It's nothing.'

'Humph! It didn't look like that to me.'

'Nothing to get into a panic about. Touch of malaria. Got it in Saudi Arabia. That's why I'm home.'

'Saudi Arabia? I thought it was Australia.'

So he was the man her father had phoned about, the one who had come home because of illness and said that he might look her up. Fancy it being Heathcliff. Yet why not? They were in the same line of business. She seemed to recall a letter some years ago from her father saying that he'd rubbed shoulders with Heathcliff—except that he called him Cliff—in his travels.

'Sorry, you've just lost me.'

'It's not important. It was a bad line. I thought Miles said Australia. Obviously I was mistaken.'

'I haven't a clue what you're talking about.'

'No, of course not.' He still looked dreadful. His color was bad, and he seemed somewhat dazed. He was, of course, still suffering the effects of his malaria attack, and this would naturally account for his confusion. She was disturbing him needlessly over a mere triviality. 'What is important is to get you comfortable,' she stated with determination.

'How do you propose to do that?' He wasn't quite back in form, but that suggestive leer was a good try.

'Now you can stop that nonsense, Heathcliff.'

'Cliff,' he said.

'Yes, Cliff.'

Suddenly, she realized she could call him Cliff and think of him by that name, as well. Heathcliff was the man who had terrified her in childhood. Miraculously, over the years, she had become a match for him, but she hadn't realized it till this moment. Seeing the chink in his armor tonight, during his attack, had done this for her. That glimpse of weakness had made him seem more approachable; he was no longer a superhuman being to cringe from in awe and fear. Perhaps more gifted than most—brains, looks, great physical strength and character—but when it got down to basics,

53

he was just an ordinary man, with man's human flaws in his makeup. He was subject to the weaknesses life inflicts on mankind just the same as every other mortal being. He was, and always would be, Cliff to her now.

'You haven't answered my question,' he said, the touch of mockery in a voice that lacked its usual vigor and sounded as shaky as he looked.

'Perhaps these will answer it for you,' she said, holding up the pajamas and sheets she'd got out in readiness.

'Stop fussing. I don't need clean pajamas and a change of sheets.'

'Of course you do. You are being stupidly stubborn. You will be much more comfortable, I assure you.'

'You are being impossibly dictatorial. I can't abide a bossy woman.'

He was scowling. He obviously liked to be thought superior to other men, above human weakness and frailties. It didn't please him at all to have his vulnerability exposed like this, but it pleased her enormously. It made a most agreeable change to have the shoe on the other foot, and she was enjoying having him at her mercy.

Giving the sleeve of his offending pajama jacket a tweak, she said: 'You wriggle out of your 'jamas while I see to the sheets. I promise not to look.'

'You vixen. I'll get you for this, I swear it.'

'Of course, if you don't feel capable of undressing yourself, I'll help,' she said, blissfully unperturbed by his threat.

'Like hell you will.'

'Tut-tut. What unexpected modesty. You've got nothing underneath that I don't know about.' It was so funny that she was almost hysterical with laughter.

The more amused she got, the less he liked it.

'If I didn't still feel groggy, I'd call your bluff, you immoral wench.'

If he hadn't looked as if he'd fall over if she as much as breathed on him, there wouldn't have been any bluff to call. She'd have been off like a rabbit out of a trap.

'I could use a glass of water,' he announced sullenly. 'My throat's so dry I feel as though I'm spitting feathers.'

'I'll get you one,' she said, and went to do just that.

She had to go downstairs for a glass. When she returned, he was sitting in the chair wearing the clean pajamas, a 'There! I hope you're satisfied' glare on his face.

She was filled with compunction for teasing him, because the effort he had expended in getting out of bed and changing had taken its toll. He looked strained again, and he was perspiring freely once more. But it had been so delicious to bait him and bring him to heel. The opportunity might never come her way again. She hoped most fervently that it wouldn't occur again under these conditions, because it smote her heart to see him suffer. On the other hand, once the situation had arisen, she hadn't been able to resist taking advantage of it.

She made up his bed for him with the clean sheets and assisted him back into it. She knew that he must be feeling as whacked as he looked, because he went as docilely as a small boy, not making any attempt to grab her and pull her down onto the bed to scare her in retaliation. Only then she found herself questioning, much to her own confusion, if it would have scared her.

Her cheeks burned as she thought of snuggling up to his hairy chest. He hadn't mustered the energy to do up the buttons on his pajama jacket, which made the fact known to her that he had a hairy chest. It was as black as the hair on his head and curled fiercely. In the situation she envisaged, she didn't think he would be wearing a pajama jacket, or the corresponding pajama bottoms, for that matter. Her skin tingled on the imagined sensation of being layered up sardine-close to him. As Cliff himself had observed previously, she had a vivid imagination, and it colored her thoughts the same rosy hue as her cheeks.

A lot of girls her age had already taken a man as their lover. Even in her immaturity she had gotten around to thinking what it would be like. Special, because she couldn't picture herself flitting from man to man like a bee going from flower to flower in search of nectar. Her body awakening to the topmost pinnacle of sensual delight, the ultimate physical pleasure. The man in her dreams had always had a virile body in peak condition but no face. Until now.

It was very strange, but she had never thought about what it would be like to go to bed with Jarvis. That had been something in the future that her mind had delicately drawn a blanket over. It came to her positively and clearly that she had never loved Jarvis. If she'd loved her ex-fiancé, the warmth and generosity of her heart wouldn't have been able to deny him the fuller relationship he had wanted. And there was something else that struck her as odd. She had always assumed as a matter of course that her heart would need to be awakened before she could give her body to a man. She didn't love Cliff. How could she? She had always held firm to the belief that love wasn't instantaneous, say, like lightning. It evolved slowly from tender beginnings. It was impossible for her to be in love so quickly. All her preconceived notions couldn't topple in one fell swoop. So, without any redeeming excuse, she felt deep humiliation and shame that she had just 'raped' Cliff in her thoughts.

He had dropped off to sleep again. She fastened the buttons on his pajama jacket, tucked the sheets back under his chin again and then, succumbing to dangerous impulse, bent down and brushed her lips across his forehead. He stirred, an unintelligible murmur escaping his lips, but he didn't waken. Her heart was beating so wildly that it seemed as though it were trying to bang its way out of her rib cage. There was a lump in her throat the size of an ostrich egg, and her legs were so shaky it was a miracle that they supported her as she tiptoed out of his room.

The next morning, she woke to the realization that she had a whopping great bruise along the curve of her cheek where Cliff had struck her when he had lashed out with his hand while she was sponging his face. Her first awareness was a painful stiffness. When she looked in the mirror, she saw it in all its discolored glory. She tried a bit of repair work, but makeup wouldn't disguise it, and it shone through regardless.

'Good heavens!' Cliff gasped when he saw it. 'A fraction higher on the cheekbone and you would have had a humdinger of a black eye. How did you come by that?'

'You should ask,' she said weakly.

'You mean I gave you that?' he inquired, aghast.

She shrugged it off. 'I bruise easily. It was my own fault. I didn't get out of the way quickly enough.'

Actually, it wasn't the only battle scar she

carried. In the struggle to cool his fevered brow, her shoulder had also gotten it. They were seated across from one another at the breakfast table, and that bruise was discreetly hidden beneath her sweater, so she had no need to let on about that.

He leaned across, and with unbelievable gentleness his fingers 'whispered' over the bruise on her face in the manner of a caress. 'I'm sorry.' A cynical but *tender* haunting of a smile came to his mouth. 'Believe me, when ladies creep into my bedroom at dead of night, that isn't the kind of treatment they can expect. On the other hand, don't believe me. Test my reactions for yourself by creeping in again tonight.'

She crunched a corner of toast between her teeth. It supplied a handy excuse for her not to speak straightaway because she didn't trust her voice.

'No, thank you. Anyway, last night my being here was a forced decision. By the time I found out that you were in residence, it was too late to seek other accommodation for myself. I don't suppose I'll be here tonight.' Was there a plea, a hint of wistfulness in her voice?

'Oh? Where will you be?'

'I haven't given it much thought as yet. The Gillybeck Arms, I suppose. I ought to stay in the area to get the mess sorted out about the repairs being done on the wrong cottage.'

'You don't have to stay in the area if you

don't want to. Any sorting out to be done, I can do. In any case, there is a perfectly simple solution to the problem. I will recompense you to the amount of the costs incurred in putting Holly Cottage in order. This will enable you to get Hawthorn Cottage done up.'

'That's very generous of you. You could, if you were so minded, make the firm, or whoever is responsible for the error, pay up.'

'I hope you're not suggesting that I would be contemptuous enough to seek personal gain from someone else's misfortune?' he inquired in frosty affront.

'Of course not. Sorry.'

'The repairs here needed doing. In getting them executed, someone has done me a favor.'

'They haven't done me much of a favor. I shall create merry hell.'

'What would that achieve? The person or persons responsible would undoubtedly get the chop. Is that what you want?'

Bristling at his taunt as indignantly as he had to hers, then rising to even greater heights of anger when she realized that his remark—unlike hers, which had been more in the way of a conjectural thought—was intended as a deliberate insult, she said, 'I hope you're not suggesting that I would be vindictive enough to want to get anyone fired, even though it was an act of gross incompetence.'

His dark, enigmatic eyes narrowed on the green flecks animating hers. 'Did you know that your eyes change color when you're angry?'

'I did,' she replied caustically. 'I wouldn't have thought you would know. Anger seems to have been the only emotion I've shown in your presence, so my eyes should have been green all the time.'

'Anger?' The suave, taunting smile that looped his mouth lassoed her breath; contriving, and almost managing, to steal it completely away. 'If that's what you really think, that all you've shown is anger, then all I can say is that you're not very good at self-analysis,' he said, at the same time flicking a hand across his forehead. It could have been to put a stray hair back in place, but it uncomfortably traced the spot where she had deposited that silly, impulsive kiss on tucking him in the night before. There was a devilish quirk running rampant across his features that marred the action too precisely for it to be coincidence.

'Aren't we deviating from the point?' Although valiantly attempting to taint her tone with cynicism, she revealed, in her sigh, her inability to get it as sharply honed as she would have wished.

The look he sent her had subtly seductive undertones that seemed to tug at her stomach muscles, drawing them in so much that once again her breathing was impaired. She really must take herself in hand. It was silly to let him affect her in that way.

'Yes, I believe we are,' he drawled. 'To return to the issue in question, and particularly to your suggestion of booking in at the Gillybeck Arms, I wouldn't if I were you. The bedrooms are immediately over the restaurant and public bar. Very noisy. Not a tranquil atmosphere at all. You'd hate it.'

Ros's small nod acknowledged that he was right.

'So let us consider the alternative. We have already agreed that I am here in the cottage by right of family ownership. Is that correct?'

'Yes,' she admitted.

'But the new chimney stack, the electrical wiring, new damp course, fitted kitchen, et cetera, et cetera, are yours. Why don't we settle for a compromise?'

'What sort of compromise?'

'Why don't we both stay here?'

'Mm,' she contemplated doubtfully.

'Unless that strikes you not so much as a compromise as a compromising situation?' She didn't much care for his play on words or his persuasiveness, for that matter, as he continued smoothly, 'Joking aside, you've always been most welcome here. My grandmother would never forgive me if I turned you out. It's not as if we are newly acquainted. The obviousness of sharing the cottage could also be described as a necessity that has been forced upon us. Perhaps your reluctance stems from last night's unfortunate happening. I'm sorry that my malaria attack frightened you. I didn't really need night nursing, so you don't have to worry on that count. I would have been perfectly all right to sweat it out on my own and will be all right in the event of it happening again. Cotton wool stuffed in your ears should do the trick.'

'I wasn't frightened. Not knowing what was happening to you made me feel inadequate. It's not that.'

'In that case, it may be that now that you have someone on hand to look after your interests—I would, you know; I would never hear the last of it from my grandmother if I didn't rise valiantly to that duty—you feel inclined to go back home. Perhaps you left things hanging fire there to be here? Work? A special man?'

She ought to have lied and said that was it. Now that she had someone reliable to leave in charge of her affairs, she could get back to the pressing needs that awaited her in both her business and personal life. Instead, she fingered her ringless engagement finger. It was a subconscious gesture she wasn't aware of until his eyes caught the action; it spoke volumes and made it so that she couldn't lie.

'There's no special man.'

'Not anymore, you mean?'

'Yes, that's what I mean. I can do my work anywhere. And I haven't a home to go to.

When I burn my boats, I truly burn 'em.'

'Like to talk about it?'

'Nothing much to talk about. I had a fiancé and a friend with whom I shared a flat. I walked in too quietly on them and—'

'Caught him with his pants down?' he queried.

'Not quite,' she said, her mouth turning wry at that figurative expression. 'Let's say I might have if I'd timed my entrance about five minutes later.'

She was glad then that she'd told him the truth.

Things were better out in the open; it had been good to tell someone, and it had seemed the most natural thing in the world for that someone to be Cliff. Odd that, because she hadn't been able to confide in Miles—whom she knew so well and trusted implicitly—the sordid details leading up to the split between her and Jarvis. At the same time, because she didn't wholly trust Cliff, she was even more delighted still that she hadn't elaborated on her truth, hadn't revealed that far from grieving over the infidelity and loss of her fiancé, she was congratulating herself on a lucky escape, because she had since realized that she had never loved him in the way one should love one's future husband. If Cliff thought she loved Jarvis and was deeply cut up about finding him in a passionate clinch with another woman, surely that would act as some kind of safeguard? A false one to be sure, but sufficient, she hoped, to protect her from the fire she would be jumping into if she agreed to share the cottage with a man she found too physically exciting, who seemed to have secured exclusive rights on her thoughts and who entranced her senses in a way no other man had ever done before.

'So there's nothing to go home to and no home to go to?'

'No.'

'You'll stay here, then,' he said, making the decision for her.

She couldn't remember actually voicing the confirming yes, but she could feel the flames licking round her toes.

## CHAPTER FOUR

He leaned forward suddenly, and the flames rose to her ankles. Her reaction—a tingling anticipation—was not lost on him, and his recognition showed in the look he then gave her—a look of sensual arrogance that knew her resistance and challenged it. He was altogether too aware of the effect he had on women, and that grated on her and steeled her determination to be the exception to the rule. In honesty, she amended her determination: to *appear* to be the exception to the rule, because she knew that deep down she was no different from the rest and that it would be all too easy to succumb to the dark enchantment of him that was holding her in thrall. She must not weaken in her resolve. She didn't like men who thought they were God's gift to women, and she wouldn't be an easy conquest. She wouldn't be a conquest at all!

'What did you think I was going to do?' he mocked softly, his eyes playing tantalizingly over her face and throat, which suddenly became constricted.

She must not swallow, because that would show how agitated she was.

'I was merely going to request that you make a fresh pot of *my* coffee on *your* stove,' he said. 'It seems to be a very sophisticated model. I hope you're worthy of it. Which is another way of instructing you that you take over that department.'

'Haven't you heard of Women's Lib? Equal shares and all that,' she demanded, piqued because he had deliberately led her to believe that he was going to do something when he had so suddenly leaned forward a moment ago.

'Heard of it. Don't much care for it. I've always regarded the kitchen as woman's territory,' he retorted indolently. 'Not that I can't turn my hand to that kind of thing in an emergency. And if I'm to base your culinary prowess on the breakfast you've just dished up,

I might well consider this to be that kind of emergency and take over.'

If that wasn't the height of injustice. So breakfast hadn't been a runaway success, She had crisped the bacon too much and broken one out of three egg yolks, but not because she wasn't a worthy cook. For heaven's sake, cooking was her business! She was regarded as a magician in the kitchen. Her cool and efficient competence and her refusal to bow to stress were invaluable assets and the guarantee that she would never be out of a job. She had turned out perfect meals of elaborate proportions in impossible conditions. At chefs' conventions, in view of the eagle eye of a rolling television camera, and at women's institutes, which perhaps confronted her with her most critical audience, she had never once had a flop. To be defeated by a meal simple enough for a schoolgirl to tackle was too unfair to be believable. And it was all his fault. As she'd gone about the task, he'd sat at the kitchen table, his eyes never leaving her. Even with her back turned, she had been aware of his lecherous appraisal.

'You were to blame for the breakfast. You shouldn't have watched me.'

'I wouldn't have thought that of you, Rusty.'

'What?'

'Latching on to a scapegoat to excuse bad workmanship.'

'That was a one-off. I'll have you know

that—' No, damn him. She wouldn't tell him. She'd show him. Would she make him eat his words before she was through!

'What?'

'Nothing,' she said sweetly, rising and walking nonchalantly over to the sink. 'I'll make that coffee you asked for. I could do with another cup myself.' Giving the implication that that was the reason she had acceded to his request. The real reason was that she'd felt the need to put some distance between them.

'Incidentally, I only brought sufficient provisions to start me off,' he called after her. 'We'll need to stock up.'

Now that she had put half the room between them, she could turn to face him again. 'You can leave that to me.'

'I intend to,' he said, his dry tone laced with derision. 'Shopping, like cooking, is woman's work.'

'In your estimation of things, woman seems to do a lot of work. What's man's work, that's what I'd like to know?'

For an answer, he took out his wallet, and from it he extracted a wad of notes that he put on the table next to her place setting. 'Man's work,' he said. 'Paying up.'

'I have money.'

'So?'

She couldn't see him letting her pay. He wasn't the type to let a woman pick up the tab.

On the other hand, it wasn't in her nature to let a man pay for her. It was bad enough to be under his roof. Even though, she thought, with a welcome return of her sense of the absurd, that roof did bear her chimney stack, she was certainly not going to let him keep her. Be a kept woman? Unthinkable!

Retracing her steps, she meticulously counted out the notes and handed half of them back to him. 'I pay for my own corn. I'll put pound for pound and keep an account of all I spend.'

'You might have grown up, but you haven't grown out of your cussedness. Even as a tot you always stood your ground, squaring your chin at me. Just as you are doing now. You had a lot of fun at my expense.'

'I did! That's a laugh. You petrified me.'

'Rubbish. You delighted in provoking me, knowing that I could only retaliate up to a point. Little did I know that my day would come.'

'Huh! Your day hasn't come,' she scoffed in negation.

'No? You're not a defenseless little girl anymore. You're a fully grown woman.' His eyes glanced over her womanly virtues: the rich curve of her bosom, obvious despite the relatively loose fit of her sweater, the narrowness of her waist, the trim, very gentle curve from hip to thigh, shown off to exquisite advantage in her tight jeans. His eyes came up slowly, relishing the return journey with undiminished enthusiasm, and looked deeply and penetratingly into hers. 'I trust that I have made my point. Now, if you get up to any provocative little tricks, you can look for a fast reprisal.'

Her breath jerked in and held an outrage. The nature of the reprisal was explicit in the smoldering, sensual promise in his eyes. Hot on the heels of that discovery came another. Why had she thought 'promise'? The obvious choice of word would have been threat.

'If you start any little tricks,' she said, gritting her teeth at him, 'you can anticipate a fast reprisal from me. I am not staying to be—'

'To be what?'

'Persecuted.'

'By what manner of feminine logic can you find anything remotely appertaining to persecution in my manner? And that's a misnomer if ever there was one. When applied to a woman, it would serve better under the heading of female folly of thinking. If there's any persecution being done, you are the one who's doing it.'

'Now by what—what *male* folly of thinking do you arrive at that conclusion?'

One kicked-back chair and two brisk strides brought him smack up in front of her. 'There was something about you that tormented me when you were a child. It hasn't lessened any now that you've grown up. In fact, it's worse, because it's a different kind of torment. I don't usually like women in jeans, but on you they look good. I still have a fancy to see you in a dress, though. You're gentle and feminine—and a complete puzzle to me,' he added, frowning darkly.

'A puzzle?'

'M'm. I can't make you out. I don't know whether you do it unconsciously or if it's deliberate. Either way, it's catastrophic.'

'What is?'

'The effect you have on me.'

'I don't know what you're talking about.'

'No? That doesn't put me off. That eggs me on. If you can't take the consequences, I'd advise you to put some distance between us.'

She didn't move. For some strange reason, she seemed to be glued to the spot. Without another word, his arms came round her. The savage swoop brought her close enough to cause her stomach muscles to contract violently at the imprint of his body. It never entered her mind to draw away from the determined descent of his mouth; not that she had much leeway for escape in the tight clamp of his arms. Her eyelashes drifted down as his lips made contact with hers, dominating them, demanding not just acquiescence but total surrender. His hands roved over her back, sending sensation after sensation coursing through her, a sweet but earthy sensuality that she had never known before.

She felt as though she were sinking under the persuasive mastery of his kiss, while at the same time being launched into a galaxy of whirling stars. More than that, she was poised on a star. It was as if she had been shown a world that she thought might exist somewhere, but she couldn't be sure. A strange, exciting place that beckoned her forward, enticing her to venture deeper into it, to sate herself fully with its delights.

Her body was melded to his by its own compulsion. Now that he didn't have to hold her fiercely to keep her close to him, his hands gently acquainted themselves with the length of her spine, teasing it with feather strokes that came up softly to subject the vulnerable spot at the back of her neck to a subtly persuasive finger caress. It achieved its purpose, triggering something off inside of her. In one small corner of her mind where common sense still prevailed, a tiny voice was imploring her not to allow herself to be manipulated in such a way. It warned that she was leaving herself wide open to hurt, but the caress was so delicious that she chose not to listen. In defiance of the voice, her arms went up round his neck, and her hands reciprocated his touch by winding into his hair and across his shoulders. The rippling strength of him tingled her fingertips. They reveled in the flexing muscles of his back as the soft curve of her mouth concurred with the insistence of his and invited a kiss that carried its vibrant sweetness down to her toes.

It ended as quickly as it had started. The arms that had brought her close still held her, but away from him. She felt so weak that if he'd let go altogether, she would have melted at his feet. Her eyes lifted slowly in the manner of someone coming out of a drugged stupor. Her mind was no quicker on the draw, so that although she was grappling with the notion that something wasn't to her liking, she couldn't make out what.

Nothing like this had ever happened to her before. It had been a wonderful trip of discovery, a dazzling experience, a surprise, a delight. But for him?

The expression on his face wiped the ecstasy from hers. Why wasn't he looking as dazed as she felt? She had expected him to look different, softer, more human. Whatever had happened to her, the experience had done nothing to knock his mantle of arrogance and mocking cynicism. In fact, he looked more complacent than ever.

She could have kicked herself for going under the spell of his dangerously handsome looks and lovemaking expertise. She had fallen for the routine finesse of a practiced charmer. He hadn't grabbed her on tender impulse or even to sate an uncontrollable urge. If passion had motivated him, she might have found it in herself to forgive him. But no! He'd done it to

73

show her that no one could hold out against him when he wished otherwise. He could congratulate himself on scoring a double victory, because as well as proving his point, he'd had a bit of fun into the bargain. She hadn't just let him; she'd bent over backward to make it extra tasty for him. She would be a long time in forgetting this humiliation—stroking his shoulders, twining her fingers into his hair, yielding her mouth to him in passionate longing, straining closer and ever closer to him. It was a wonder he'd managed to keep from laughing. How could she have been so stupid? She had sensed there was danger, but not the extent of it, and in her ignorance she had thought she could handle it.

'Why did you have to go and do a silly thing like that for?' she demanded, her anger vented as much at herself as against him.

'Didn't you enjoy it?'

'A snake bite would have been preferable.'

'What's smarting you?'

'As if you didn't know.'

'I think you're being slightly absurd. It wasn't as if I didn't warn you beforehand. You got exactly what you asked for.'

'Is that so? Well, let me tell you something. Whatever else you think you've accomplished, you've just made it impossible for me to stay here with you.'

'Grow up, Rusty. Fool me for thinking that you already had,' he jeered. 'You're only a

74

woman on the outside. Inside you're still a cringing child. What's more, you haven't the spunk you had when you were a child. The child you were wouldn't have run away from any situation, no matter how fraught. She would have faced up to it. Even if she was frightened, she'd have died rather than show it.'

'I hope you're not suggesting that I'm frightened of you.'

'Actually, I wasn't.'

'That's as well. I don't trust you, but I'm not frightened of you.'

'Lies make poor weapons, especially when one lies to oneself. I think it's fairly obvious, without my having to labor the point, that I've never needed to take a woman against her will. And I'm not about to start now. It's not me you don't trust, Rusty. You don't trust yourself with me, and there is the subtle difference. How is it when a woman feels unsure of herself, she lashes out at some poor guy? All women are the same.'

Writhing at the unjustness of that contemptuous accusation, she flung at him, 'All men aren't the same, I'm thankful to say. I've never met one in your mold before. You're bitter and cynical and full of your own importance.'

His eyes flicked over her with scorn. 'All, this because of a few meaningless kisses? I don't believe it!' His manner veered between aggression and ridicule as he challenged coldly: 'Or weren't those kisses meaningless on your part? Was that soft mouth beneath mine searching for more than sensuous pleasure?'

'What pleasure? If you got any you were lucky. I derived none.'

For a second, their glances clashed in silent antagonism.

Then a soft, derisive 'No-o?' spilled slowly from his lips.

A thought occurred to her. 'I can understand why I feel as I do. I've every right to object to being pawed, but for the life of me, I can't understand your attitude.' She expected him to take her up on accusing him of pawing her, but his frown grooved deeper, and the notion came to her that he had a bigger issue to ponder on, although it beat her what it could be. 'What are you getting uptight about?' she demanded to know.

But was uptight the right word? Wasn't there something on the defensive about his manner? What was he backing away from?

He was glaring at her as if she were the guilty party and not the other way round. She didn't know how it had come about; it certainly wasn't of her skillful maneuvering, because she had been swept along by the tide of events, but somehow she had managed to get under his skin.

Even as she struggled to understand his attitude, she tried not to be intimidated by it.

Or by the virile strength that radiated from his body and had such an enervating effect on her, putting her into a state totally beyond the scope of her experience.

Experience! That was a laugh. The intensity and depth of his kisses had brought it forcibly home to her that in comparison to the girls he was used to dealing with, she could award herself a nil rating. She'd only been dancing along the fringes of lovemaking with Jarvis. No wonder he'd strayed. And thank goodness he had. She might have gone through life thinking that milk-and-water kisses were all there was to it. She had a lot to be grateful to Jarvis for. In not being satisfied with what she had to give, he had done her a favor, even though he was responsible for her present predicament. Because the fire she had stepped into was now licking above her knees.

Throughout all this, he had kept hold of her wrists; suddenly, he levered her forward. Her body was just short of touching his. His breath scorched her cheek; his nearness seared her senses. She tried to dismiss it as mere sexual excitement, knowing there was nothing mere about it. It was explosive. So close, too close, not close enough. She ought to freeze against him, but she was a yielding fire, a humiliation to herself and her fine intentions to stay aloof. She fought to regain control of herself, knowing that his eyes were playing over her face, drinking in the startling clarity of the emotions expressed there. She had never been much good at covering up, and the feelings stirring within her were too new for her to have found the key to regulate them at this stage. She needed time.

Her mouth was dry with tension. She pressed her lips together to moisten them. Her emotions weren't obedient to her will but subservient to the strange power he seemed to have over her. She wasn't her own mistress, but she'd be damned if she would be his!

'Let go of me!'

'Your eyes aren't saying that.'

'Can I help it if I have stupid eyes? Look, Cliff, be fair. This isn't in the deal.'

'Deal?'

'Commitment we've made, if you want to parry words.'

'You're off beam, Rusty. A physical need was expressed, but no commitment was made.'

'What in heaven's name are you talking about? You're the one who's off beam. I was referring to the commitment we've made to share your cottage until mine's been made habitable. It isn't going to work unless you step smartly back into line. I'll do the cooking—I don't mind filling your stomach—but I'm not going to fill your bed.'

'Are you always so plain spoken?' His face mirrored strong disapproval. 'Some things aren't put into words.'

So he didn't like plain speaking. She'd

78

managed to get under his skin again, but this time she knew the cause and mentally filed what could be a useful piece of information.

'All I can say is, they should be,' she retorted airily, before snapping: 'Stop being so damned superior. I can spout the social niceties along with the rest when I want to. As for the other—'

'What other?'

'The self-opinionated implication that every woman is out to trap you into matrimony.'

'How do you know that I haven't been trapped? How do you know that I'm not married? At my age, the majority of men are.'

'I don't know.' Her eyes swung sharply up to his. 'Are you?'

'No. And not about to be.'

'Are we getting down to the nitty-gritty? The whole point of this demonstration. You're not averse to accepting anything that might be an offer, but it won't end with a short walk down the aisle. It'll be, "So long, been nice knowing you." A hail and a farewell affair, with no strings—or should that be rings—attached. Oh, I'm sorry,' she said with saccharine sweetness, 'I forgot your aversion to plain speaking. I must remember that some things aren't put into words.'

'On this occasion, I've no quibble with your plain speaking. It's better that you know how things stand.'

She didn't like the way he'd put the onus on

her. She looked pointedly down at the hands still binding her wrists. 'You also know how things stand, Cliff.'

'Precisely.'

This round was hers, but she felt no sense of victory as he dropped her wrists and walked away.

He was cool and shrewd and too damned confident that eventually he'd get what he wanted. She wasn't at all sure that it wasn't what she wanted, too. But why had he tried to rush her? Why, instead of acting as if there weren't a moment to lose, hadn't he taken it in nice and easy courtship stages? Then she laughed at her own reasoning. 'Courtship' was the last word applicable. It went with that other word beginning with C—commitment. Either marriage or that other arrangement that is becoming exceedingly popular with a certain set these days, the commitment of a deep and meaningful relationship.

At heart, Ros still clung to orange-blossom dreams. Rice and rings and saving the top tier of the wedding cake for the first special event. Yet she took the realistic view that sometimes things prevented couples from marrying. She knew of heartbreaking circumstances when it was right for a couple to live together as man and wife without going through the sanctity of the ceremony. If the affections were deep enough, she thought that heaven, in its mercy, would overlook the odd earthly lapse. But she couldn't condone two people coming together, with no thoughts of making it a permanency, to appease an of-the-moment, selfish physical urge. Even though the sexual excitation he had aroused in her was as rife as ever. She went weak just thinking of his strong arms around her, his lips leading her into bliss, the tantalizing nearness of his body acting like an apéritif to her hormones. Yet she couldn't see herself consenting to being everything to him. Not unless there was some compelling reason.

\*      \*      \*

After dealing with the breakfast dishes, Ros went shopping. Cliff was going to seek out the agent and sort him out to get things moving as regarded the repairs required to make Hawthorn Cottage habitable again.

Ros knew that she wouldn't be able to get everything she needed in Gillybeck, and she didn't even try. She drove farther afield to a town with the kind of shops that she knew would cater to her specialized requirements. It wasn't just a case of proving herself to Cliff; she needed certain ingredients for experimental recipes that she intended to try out for the book she was writing.

She piled her purchases into the trunk of her car and decided she was in no desperate hurry to return to the cottage. Cliff could scratch up his own lunch. She wasn't going to feel domestic toward him. She'd undertaken those duties, but she didn't have to carry them to extremes. She'd only agreed to take on the cooking because it suited her purpose to do so.

She enjoyed a late, leisurely lunch in a popular restaurant. Usually, when she dined out, her working brain took an interest in the food, but she ate without really tasting anything and afterward couldn't remember what she'd eaten. A man sitting at a table nearby tried to pick her up; she wasn't even aware of it. Her mind was preoccupied with Cliff. She couldn't stop thinking about how ill he had been during the night. He still hadn't looked one hundred percent fit that morning, but considering how bad he'd been, he'd made a fantastic recovery. He'd said it was malaria. She'd always dismissed that as something of little consequence, an attack of shivers that she'd supposed would be mildly uncomfortable. She hadn't realized what a violent effect it could have on a person or how frightening it was to observe. He had gone through all the stages of gray and green; and even that morning, although his fantastic suntan had disguised it to a certain extent, his color still hadn't been back to normal. He wouldn't lie to her about the nature of his illness, surely? What would be the point? It would be malaria if that's what he said it was. So what was nagging at her?

After lunch, she decided to look round the

shops again, but this time not the ones that sold only food. There was a festive look about the windows, a reminder that Christmas was slightly less than two weeks away. In the hustle, she'd forgotten. How could anyone forget the approach of Christmas, for goodness' sake?

To make up for her forgetting, she bought some Christmassy things. Crackers and decorations, a bright shining silver star and tree baubles and the special sweetmeats that were a must at that time of the year. She bought herself a Christmas dress in soft red wool. Redheads can't normally wear red, but careful choice of the shade of red and the cooling quality of her gray eyes meant that she could. She would have liked to buy a present for Cliff, but nothing seemed appropriate, so eventually she gave up the search. Perhaps she would find something suitable somewhere else, possibly even in Gillybeck, nearer the date.

The extra shopping and dawdling meant that she was much later in getting back to Holly Cottage than she'd intended. The turnoff road she took was ink dark, but because Cliff hadn't drawn the curtains, the square of light from the window was a bright yellow welcoming beacon that she raced to eagerly despite the potholed road.

The door opened as she jumped out of the car. The doorways of country cottages are noted for their smallness, and Cliff's tall frame filled the limited space. The most ridiculous urge came over her to run to him, to be swept off her feet and enfolded in his arms. His unwelcoming growl firmly repressed it.

'You've been a long time,' he said. 'I thought you'd decided not to come back.'

Is that what he'd wanted? Had he hoped that she would spend the day thinking things out and subsequently reach the conclusion that the arrangement of sharing a cottage was unsuitable, after all, and not bother to return?

'I didn't have much option. All my things are here, aren't they?' she said, jerking a disdainful chin at him before going to the trunk.

As Cliff carried in the mammoth supply of groceries, she wished she hadn't bought so lavishly. It looked as though she were preparing for a siege or contemplating staying for a long, long time. As for the Christmas stuff, it was as if someone else had bought those. A bright, happy spirit in no way related to the dejected girl who scooped up the various boxes and parcels with casual indifference.

# CHAPTER FIVE

The evening meal fell short of her capabilities. Time was short, but that was not the cause, because she'd allowed for that and prepared something quick and uncomplicated. Kebabs of lamb with spiced orange sauce and saffron rice. The lamb was inclined to be tough, and the rice was not as fluffy as she would have liked. The fact that this dish, like the breakfast, wouldn't have tested the capabilities of a schoolgirl overmuch made it all the more exasperating. What now for her brave challenge of the morning to make him eat his words?

It wouldn't have been so bad if he'd been scornful. He was impossibly nice; nice for him, anyway. There was only a faintly cynical gleam in his eye as he said: 'Never mind, Rusty. Some girls are born cooks; others are born to be decorative.'

It was the kind of backhanded compliment she could have done without. In fact, she didn't realize there was any compliment there, even though she had taken the trouble to change out of her jeans into a dress and brushed her hair out, until she sifted the words about in her mind later.

Then she glared at him and said, 'I am an excellent cook.'

He collected a sticky mound of rice onto his fork. 'That is a matter of opinion.'

'I know this doesn't say so. But I *am*. This is not representative of what I can do.'

'Oh, sure. Gremlins in the kitchen. Or perhaps the stove is faulty?'

'There's nothing the matter with the stove, as you well know. You might be right about the other. At least, not gremlins—one gremlin.'

'So you're blaming me again, are you?'

'No. As you so rightly pointed out this morning, bad workmanship shouldn't be blamed on bad tools or anything else. I've cooked before more exacting audiences than you and haven't flapped. I'll get the dessert,' she said, rising from her chair and sending him a cool, challenging look that was not without its spike of humor. 'You don't have to worry; it's fruit salad, and all I had to do was open the can. And cheese and biscuits. Likewise, I can be trusted not to make a mess of that.'

It was silly, but the gremlin theory was not entirely without credibility. The fact was, he put her off. Her awareness of him seemed to have stolen her ability to do even the simplest tasks.

Even the coffee wasn't up to her normal standard, but it provided a more relaxed atmosphere in which to talk. If being with someone who was physically exciting can ever be described as relaxed. It was balm to her

86

self-esteem that he seemed as inclined as she was to tarry and chat. At first, about impersonal things—books, records, films, gaduating to old times. He didn't once mention her father. She might have thought that was odd, as he'd been working with him so recently, but for the fact that, as now, her father hadn't been around much in the old days. She must remember to ask Cliff how her father was getting on, but there was no desperate hurry. If anything had been amiss, he would have told her. When people don't say anything, it's because there's nothing to tell, or perhaps Cliff might think the antics her father got up to weren't right for a daughter's ears, she realized with a rueful, inner laugh.

Being so much older than she was, Cliff remembered her mother very well, which was a delight to her. It was one of Ros's big regrets that her mother had died before she'd had time to appreciate her. She sometimes wondered if she would even have remembered her face if the handful of old photogaphs that she had in her possession and frequently looked at hadn't kept her mother's dear face vivid in her memory. As Cliff drew a verbal picture for her, she could have sat and listened all night, and to this end she swallowed back a couple of yawns. The third one wouldn't be suppressed, however, and on observing it, Cliff declared that it was time they turned in.

As they went up the stairs together, the

amiability they had shared went the opposite way. Ros was jittery, on edge. It didn't make sense, because when a man and woman are attracted to one another, any room, any place—lonely country lane, the back seat of a car—is a danger zone. There is as much temptation in a downstairs room as an upstairs one; the upstairs room only seems more hazardous, that's all. If he'd wanted to pounce on her, he would have done so when they were close in mood, not now that she'd gone away from him. He wouldn't try to penetrate the icy front she'd put up. Unless he saw it as a form of provocation. A 'don't touch' with a dare in its tail.

She sneaked a sideways glance at him and hoped that he hadn't misconstrued her reasons for being there. Why do the hours of darkness cast a bewitching spell, while everything seems adult and logical during the hours of daylight? It had seemed such a sensible solution to share.

'What's the matter?' he asked, puzzled.

Or was he only pretending to be puzzled? There seemed to be a veiled invitation in his manner for her to resort to her penchant for plain speaking. His cunning would get him nowhere. No way was she going to bring this out into the open. If she admitted to anything, it would be as good as asking him into her bedroom. On this issue, both her mouth and her bedroom door were going to stay closed to him.

'Nothing,' she said, shrugging in a manner that she hoped would convey indifference. 'Guess it's been a long day and I'm tired.'

'Yes,' he said, his little finger so gently touching the delicate area under her eye, a mere feather stroke. 'Those shadowed crescents shouldn't be there.' But the expression in his eyes was not in agreement with his words and asserted that tiredness was not the cause of her jumpiness.

How aware was he of the duel going on inside of her: her wish that she could have an easier attitude toward sex clashing with her insistence that it wasn't right in the absence of deeper feelings? To use the body for gratification without love was like drinking vintage champagne from an earthenware mug. To be fully appreciated, wine should be sipped from the finest hand-cut crystal, and sex shouldn't be to satisfy lust but to consummate the most tender and beautiful relationship known to mankind, the love between a man and a woman. A love so selfless that it almost reaches spiritual heights as it touches physical depths. A bodily union that encompasses the soul.

She knew that if she took one step forward, his arms would open to form the protective circle she wanted to walk into. Wanted it so badly that it jarred something inside. Her stomach muscles were tense in their pain. An ache of sweetness and vibrant intensity filled her throat. Her body was in the grip of some sweeping cataclysm; her mind was in a state of total confusion, yet running through it was a tiny thread of common sense. He would not be satisfied with having his arms around her to give—and glean—comfort for what was denied, and if she were honest with herself, neither would she. There was a hot thirsting passion between them that demanded to be slaked. A wonderful torment that was like an emotional whip that wouldn't stop cracking until their bodies were lashed together—in what? It had to be a commitment, not lust. It always came back to that. She would not satisfy his lust.

She took the vital step, the step toward self-dignity, which was the step away from him.

'Good night,' she said, her chin high as she swept into her room.

'Pleasant dreams,' he called after her, his voice pitched into sardonic darkness and cruel mockery.

Once inside her door, she leaned her hot cheek against the cold closed panel. It should have been his muscled chest. Just to think of being crushed close to his powerful body took the strength from her legs and turned her insides to water again. She resented his magnetism, and she was bitterly ashamed of her own response. She had to cram her fist against her mouth to stop herself from calling out to him. She knew that he hadn't moved and that he was standing on the other side of the door. He was waging a war on her nerves as well as her emotions. She didn't know how long she was going to be able to hold out . . . how long she would want to hold out.

As though blocking the door, she stayed where she was until he moved away—a gesture of defense that was meaningless because he wouldn't have pushed his way in but would only have entered by invitation. As his footsteps faded along the passage, she dragged her weak legs over to the bed where she collapsed, her thoughts in a dizzy turmoil. What was the matter with her? She was acting completely out of character. It wasn't like her to abandon herself in this stupid fashion, to give way to emotional lunacy. With these hectic thoughts, she dropped off to sleep.

The next morning, she bounced back, her normal almost-in-control self. She knew the control was not total when she again made a hash of the breakfast. If she hadn't been so irritated by the injustice of it all, she might have been quite amused.

The omelets she whipped up for lunch were a dream. But the goulash she made for the evening meal was so fiery it was like swallowing flames.

She gave Cliff points for eating it with apparent relish and without comment. She was, however, somewhat nonplussed, because she sensed what the follow-up question would be when he asked conversationally, 'I believe you said you wrote books?'

She would like to have denied ever having made that rash statement, but as she had spent the day closeted in the front parlor with her typewriter, she couldn't.

'Yes, I do,' she said.

Right on cue, he asked: 'What kind of book are you writing?'

If she said a cookbook, she could imagine the meal of hilarity he would make of that.

'It—er—sort of advises women on how to catch their man.' On pondering about it, she supposed that hadn't been a very inspired reply. If anything, it was worse than admitting to the dreadful truth.

'You've got to be joking.'

'Have I?' she inquired with disarming sweetness.

'And you feel qualified to do this?' he said, cynicism biting deep in his smoky eyes. 'If any publisher is unwise enough to publish it, be sure to send me an autographed copy.'

Her bristling defense came back with pleasing swiftness and matched the haughtiness of her tone. 'I'll do better than that. I'll put a special dedication in it for you.'

She already knew what that dedication would say. 'Eat your words, Cliff.' She'd like to make him eat his words on both counts—on her cooking prowess and on her ability to catch her man. The man, of course, being him.

She dared not meet his gaze in case he read this last wistful reflection in her eyes.

When he replied, the lazy indolence in his tone whipped her, yet it also was not without a reflective quality that she found oddly surprising. 'I would have thought that any reasonably gifted female wouldn't have any difficulty in catching her man,' he said. 'Men like to think of themselves as the hunter, but it's an indisputable fact that they are prey to a woman's allure. But allure is a strange, mystic thing. In my experience, it wears off. Once a man has been enticed—'

'Got what he wants, you mean,' she snapped back sarcastically, giving full rein to her blunt tongue.

'If you care to put it so crudely, yes. A woman then becomes less alluring.'

'That is a very cynical viewpoint.'

'Maybe it's my misfortune, but it's the only one I've been given.'

'Don't you believe that a man can find a satisfying, lasting relationship with a woman?'

'I must. Otherwise, I wouldn't keep looking.'

Latching on to the implication of that, she said, 'And in the search, somewhere along the line, someone is going to get hurt. As your feelings are never sufficiently involved, it isn't going to be you. It will have to be the poor cast-off female. I hope you meet your match. By the law of averages, you're going to come up against a girl who finds you less alluring on acquaintance and gives you the big elbow. I just hope I'm around to see it. But I doubt that very much. I don't think you are capable of the kind of deep affection that goes with a lasting involvement. Well, just watch it. You aren't going to be a devastating thirty-two-year-old forever with a convoy of girls ready to fall into your arms. Time could be running out for you.'

As she jumped up from the table and stalked away on that note of victory, she couldn't know how bitterly she was going to regret saying those words.

He followed her and caught up with her by the door, grabbing her wrists and bringing her round to face him, his dark eyes glowering. 'You little fool. Don't you realize that I know all this already. I'm trying my best not to hurt you.'

'Your consideration bowls me over.'

'And so it should, seeing as you're not worthy of it. To make this crazy arrangement of sharing a home work, even short-term, you've got to play your part. A casual affair with a girl I knew in pigtails and ankle socks is out of the question, especially when the girl has only thrown away the outer trappings of childhood. I'm not that much of a heel. But stop tempting me; otherwise—'

'What?' she challenged rashly, incensed by his uncomplimentary opinion of her.

His lashes closed, reducing his eyes to slits.

'I'm only human, Rusty. Bearing this in mind, I'm sure your vivid imagination can be relied upon to draw its own torrid conclusions.'

\*     \*     \*

She hardly saw Cliff the next week. She wasn't sure whether that was by design or circumstance, possibly a combination of both. He explained his absences with plausibility. A hospital checkup took him into town and necessitated an overnight stay. 'Strictly routine company policy,' he had assured her on seeing her wide-eyed look of alarm. Another two days, with three overnight stays, was essential to some business that needed his attention. Perhaps it was legitimate and not put-up excuses to keep out of her way.

She used the time well and made great strides with her book. Like the ones that had gone before it, it wasn't just a compilation of recipes. She slipped in enough text to make it a witty and informative read. It was said that more people bought Rosalynd Seymour cookbooks to read than to cook by. A droll smile came to her lips as she thought what Cliff would have made of that. In her head, she could almost hear the cynicism in the imaginary voice of Cliff as he said, 'Judged on the efforts you've served up for me, that's just as well.'

The frustrating part of it was, now that he

wasn't here to cook for, she had regained her skills. Everything she turned out achieved a peak of perfection. In a very busy schedule, she also found time to bake a Christmas cake that she had decorated with a roughed-up snow scene. She wondered if it would snow for Christmas. She hoped so. Up there in that remote area, snow transformed it into a white fairytale world that was frequently cut off from the rest of civilization. It was cold enough for it, and snow was forecast. She wondered if Cliff would be spending Christmas with her at the cottage—or would he make some souped-up excuse to stay away?

He arrived back just as an early dusk was falling on December the twenty-third. Her heart lifted so high she wondered how it managed not to catapult her to the ceiling.

'Business go okay?' she asked, gripping her hands tightly behind her back and feigning indifference at seeing him.

'M'm . . . satisfactory, thank you. Have you been all right?'

'Of course.'

'Thought I'd better get back. Snow is forecast.'

'So I heard on the radio.'

'The Gillybeck Arms is putting on a dinner dance tonight. I tentatively booked a table. If we're not there by eight-thirty, I left instructions for the staff to let it go. What do you say?'

What was this all about? Was there any significance in the fact that he was taking her on a date?

'The chef is putting on a Christmas dinner. I thought it would save you the bother of cooking this evening, unless you're already mutilating something in the oven, that is? And at the same time, it will ensure that we get one decent festive meal.'

She could cheerfully have hit him. So much for the tender thought that he had returned to court her. As for the implication she'd got on following the thread of that terse conversation —that he had made sure he got back before it snowed because he didn't like to think of her alone here and possibly cut off—well, that was equally ludicrous. That didn't negate the fact that it would be good to put a slinky dress on and have a night of fun and frivolity, and she wasn't going to cut off her nose to spite her face by turning the offer down.

'Sounds fine by me,' she said in acceptance, carefully keeping the enthusiasm out of her voice as her mind planned ahead what to wear.

Later that day, she considered the two evening gowns that were equally dressy and suitable for the occasion. Her face was pink from soaking in the luxury of a perfumed bath, and still she couldn't decide between the slip of a green dress, which—what little there was of it—molded to her figure, while the metallic thread running through it turned it to silver in

97

certain lights, or the just as lovely, if frigidly demure, ice blue.

The hand of prudence would have come down on the ice blue, but with reckless daring, Ros's fingers finally pulled the slippery green material over her head. What its color did for her burnished hair, the dress did for her figure. It needed little enhancement, and Ros dipped lightly into her jewelry box for a fine silver chain that encircled her throat and emphasized the slashing low cut of her neckline. The dress breathed sensuality, and as a token to decorum, she wound her hair back in a staid coil, even though she remembered that Cliff had once told her he liked it loose best. She was more extravagant with her eye shadow than normal—on the rare occasions she wore it, she preferred just a smear across her lids; and the same abandoned hand splashed on her favorite evening perfume, which gave out a rich and heady fragrance and added just the right wickedly decadent note.

As she walked down the stairs, Cliff stood in the lower hall, his eyes waiting to ambush her. They didn't so much stalk her as absorb every particle of her, her hair, her forehead, her shining, frantically striving to be guarded eyes, the soft pinkness of her mouth, her working throat. And down, concentrating for endless moments on the well-defined hollow of her cleavage and the rising fullness of her breasts, revealed to him by the cut of her dress. It was odd, but there hadn't seemed quite as much of her exposed in her bedroom mirror as there was now as seen through his eyes.

Without lifting his glance, he said: 'Pity that old-fashioned custom of buying a corsage for a lady has lost its popularity. The difficulty I would have encountered in knowing where to pin it would have been offset by the fun of trying.'

He was rubbing the thumb and forefinger of one hand together. It was a gesture that displayed his own inner tension and was without ulterior motive. He could not know what it did to her. A shiver ran through her as though his thumb were not rotating on his own finger, but on a part of her body that her dress did not bare to him. It was a relief when his gaze slid farther down, going no lower than a faintly protruding hipbone before returning to her by now flushed face.

'Very lovely. Very elegant. You look taller. The transformation has measured you more up to my size.'

That was not strictly true, although her precariously high heels meant that he didn't have to look as far down to locate her eyes. But of course he wasn't referring to her height at all. He meant that she now measured up to his level of sophistication.

'Are you ready?'

For what? she wondered as she picked up her evening wrap and nodded in silent consent.

*　　　*　　　*

A tall, heavily branched Scotch pine tree dominated the entrance hall. Another stood in the corner of the room where the dinner dance was being held, its towering branches laden with baubles and blazing with Christmas lights. Crackling logs shot flames up the wide chimney of a fireplace that was huge enough to walk into, and a three-piece orchestra was playing Christmas carols. Silver garlands looped above their heads, and streamers and other party novelties decorated each table. The one the head waiter led them to was at the far end of the room on the edge of the dance floor.

Ros gulped on laughter as she feasted her eyes on the blazing gaiety of the room. Her happiness overflowed and showed in the exuberance of her smile. As the last notes of a popular carol faded away, Ros put her hands together and clapped louder than anyone else, but whether she was paying homage to the musicians or clapping for the sheer joy of being there with Cliff was difficult to tell.

There were variations on the menu, but both she and Cliff stuck to the traditional Christmas fare. Couples had taken to the floor between courses, but so far they hadn't joined them. It wasn't until twin glasses of brandy sat

100

alongside the coffee cups that Cliff asked her if she would care to dance. She nodded and went into his arms on a blissful sigh of contentment. They'd had little to drink, just a glass of wine with the meal and then a few sips of brandy, but the people around them had imbibed freely; and streamers whirled in the air with cast-off inhibitions.

Gathering her closer, he did not talk, and both of those things suited Ros. She wanted to imprint the lovely evening on her memory for all time. Oddly, in the midst of her enjoyment, a thread of unease ran through her mind. There was an inexplicable bittersweet quality about everything. Later, she was to ask herself if, by some uncanny instinct, she had perceived some inkling of what was in store for her.

Normally, her head would have rested against the steel wall of his chest; but her higher heels enabled it to fit in the curve of his neck. The hand on her back rested just above the line where her dress ended. The trespassing tip of his little finger strayed possessively beneath the material, while on the higher level, his stroking thumb shivered over her bare skin. His other hand clasped hers and was crushed between their bodies. The back of his hand rested on her breast, again just slightly to the side of where her dress ended, so that his knuckles burned like a branding iron on her sensitized flesh. She never, never, never wanted the music to end. She wanted to stay forever in his arms, held so cherishingly close.

They stayed until the delicious end, not leaving until the early hours of December the twenty-fourth. Christmas Eve morning was just two hours old, and feathers of snow touched their faces as, arms linked round waists, they walked to the car.

'I hope it comes down thick and fast and everywhere is covered by snow in the morning,' Ros declared.

'Not too densely covered, I hope. There are things to be done. Holly to be collected and a tree to be brought in.'

'I got the trimmings when I went shopping for the food,' Ros volunteered happily.

They entered Holly Cottage, and their feet pointed of one accord to the kitchen. Ros abandoned her wrap and tipped milk into a saucepan, to be heated on the stove for a hot bedtime drink. Cliff leaned against the counter and watched her. The strange brooding look on his face did not fit in with the atmosphere of the evening. Inevitably, the milk boiled over.

They cleaned up the mess together and decided not to bother with a bedtime drink. Cliff put his hands up to her hair, and two deft flicks brought its brightness tumbling over his fingers. Was that why she'd worn it in that style, not to 'cool' the look of her dress but to tempt Cliff to remove the restraining pins, as he had once before?

He cupped her face in his hands, and he kissed her not urgently on the lips, although his expression was still strange. Then he turned her round and bade her a firm good night.

She went up to her room, not altogether knowing why she had been sent away, yet knowing that it was right for him not to rush things between them. The pace, at first, had been too hectic, but now it was right for it to slow down and take its own course.

If only she knew the reason for this funny little pain under her heart. She had the oddest feeling that the price she was going to be asked to pay for her happiness would be too cruel to bear. It was uncanny how she knew that it was soon to be partnered by a sorrow that would drag her down into depths of misery and torment that, in her wildest fears, she had never thought to experience.

## CHAPTER SIX

The next morning, Ros's eyes opened to a dazzling brightness, and she knew that her wish had been granted. She flew to the window and saw that it had snowed through the night. Not only was the landscape a different color, but it was also a different shape. White trees took on odd dimensions. The sun had come out as though marking its approval, and the blue-white glare of the rolling hills sparkled in the grip of a million dancing sunbeams.

As she surveyed the frosty, bejeweled scene, a white wonderland, her gloom of the previous day completely disappeared. It was a day to lift one's face up to in bright optimism. Every moment was too precious to squander on despondent fears that lurked in, and were the product of, some dark and obscure pocket of the imagination and had no substance.

She pulled on trousers and a thick sweater, knowing that with those tucked under her sheepskin coat, she would be cozy and warm when they went out after breakfast in search of a tree and boughs of evergreen. It was unthinkable not to have holly in Holly Cottage at Christmas. And . . . perhaps . . . mistletoe.

Similarly muffled to his chin, Cliff had started on the breakfast. Despite his opinion of her cooking, he made no demur when she waded in to help. When the washing up was done, they put on coats and scarfs, and Ros dug out a woolly cap with a pompon that matched her scarf, and out they went.

They didn't hang about but marched at a brisk pace. Cliff, who had been on many a similar mission in years past, knew exactly where to look, and it wasn't long before they were dragging their spoils back and dumping them by the kitchen door.

Ros was kicking the snow off her boots by the door in preparation for entering when a snowball glanced by her cheek. She immediately retaliated, and for the next half hour they indulged in a boisterous snowball fight. Cliff's aim might have been the better, but he was the kinder, and so his person was spattered with more white blobs than hers. Her cheeks burned with the cold and the exhilaration, and when they did eventually fall through the kitchen door, they brought ravenous appetites with them. She had made a casserole the day before that only needed heating up. It was more than just good, it was excellent, but Cliff wolfed his plateful down without comment. It's an annoying trait in people, but when something is right, it's taken for granted that it should be and passes without attracting attention. It's only when it's wrong that it gets noticed.

She made mince pies, and again these were up to her usual standard. This time Cliff did comment. On tasting one, he asked by what fluke she had managed it.

'Could it be that you weren't watching me?' she said sweetly.

He had been busy potting the tree and festooning the living room with holly and the sprig of mistletoe she'd seen him collect. As yet, she had no idea where it lurked, but when she found out, she had every intention of standing under it.

She brought out the silver garlands and the tree ornaments she had purchased, and their joint efforts soon had the tree dressed in the Christmas spirit. The star that she had saved for the top defeated her. She expected Cliff to take it from her fingers and his long reach to achieve what she couldn't; instead, he placed a hand on either side of her waist and lifted her up. She strained over his shoulder and fixed the star in place and was then brought back down to her feet. The descent was slow and fraught with tense excitement as she slithered the length of his long frame. There was a febrile pause in the procedure as their eyes drew level. The brooding intensity her eyes read in his clogged her throat. It had been a fun day, sparkling with joy and ecstasy, but throughout she had caught passing glimpses of much the same look that was on his face now. She knew that he wanted to kiss her, wanted to do more than kiss her. It was there, a torment straining his features and clenching his jaw. But he denied himself the opportunity, just as he had been ignoring opportunity all day, and set her unkissed on her feet.

As his hands left her waist, her eyes dropped to the floor, and she saw two gift-wrapped packages, both bearing her name, under the tree. She put the mystery of why Cliff was acting as he was behind her and concentrated on the dismaying fact that she still hadn't gotten a present for him. Her eyes

106

raced to the clock. There was still time. If she got a move on, she would get into Gillybeck before the shops shut. Shops were limited, and so choice would be, too. She hoped that one of the two shops that specialized in gifts and souvenirs would have something suitable.

She would have to take her car, because it was too far to walk, even though driving conditions might be precarious because of ice and the possibility of snowdrifts.

'I've just remembered something I want from the village,' she explained to Cliff as she went to retrieve her boots from the corner of the kitchen where she'd stepped out of them.

'Whatever it is, can't it wait?'

'No, it can't.'

'If it's that urgent, I'll fetch it for you.'

'Honestly, all this fuss,' she mocked. 'I'm a careful driver. Anyway, you couldn't go for me. As well as getting something I've forgotten, I want to make a phone call. There's someone I'd like to wish a happy Christmas to.'

'Oh! Sorry if I'm being obtuse.'

His stiff tone told her that he thought she wanted to slip out by herself to phone Jarvis. Perhaps he thought that was the whole object of her going and that the other, wanting to get something before the shops closed, was a trumped-up excuse. Actually, it was Miles she had a notion to ring. But she didn't want company, certainly not *his* company while she chose *his* present, so it was better to let him

107

think what he did. Besides which, she was wallowing in a thought that was almost too delicious to believe, and if she did believe it, then it seemed to her advantage to keep the pot boiling on that one for a while longer.

'You're jealous!' she accused with taunting sweetness.

'What an absurd thing to say,' he scoffed. The dash of anger in his eyes coupled with the searing dryness of his tone told her that she was not far off the mark.

He left the kitchen in a huff, and she was already sorry for drawing him out. With regret, she had to watch him go. She would have gone after him if time hadn't been at a premium. As it was, she pulled on her boots and shrugged her arms into her coat.

It had started to snow again. She hadn't been driving long before she realized that it had been a mistake to venture out on any errand, no matter how pressing, on such a day. At first, the fall of snow was moderate, but it increased from a pretty spectacle into a venomous attack. She gripped the steering wheel and leaned forward, her eyes aching from the effort of trying to penetrate a swirling cloud of whiteness. The wind whipped the flakes onto the windshield faster than the wipers could whisk them off.

It crossed her mind to wonder why she didn't turn back, why she was so dedicated to going on. The thought of phoning Miles had triggered something off in her brain. The last time she'd phoned him, on her arrival, he had told her that Cliff had been working with her father and that he was home on sick leave and intended to look her up. Miles had attempted to tell her something about Cliff, but the static on the line had been so bad that every time he had tried, his voice had been drowned out. It now seemed imperative for her to know what Miles had said. It just might be something that would help her to understand Cliff's strange manner. The foreboding that had been with her the previous night was back again. She wasn't going to find any peace until she knew what it was all about. If Miles could tell her anything, anything at all . . .

The car began to slide out of her control. Her first immediate impulse was to step on the brakes, but she managed to temper that reaction. She remembered in time that that was the last thing she must do if she wanted to keep out of trouble. She bit hard on her lip, willing herself not to panic, and somehow found the strength of mind to do all the right things to get the car out of the spin. Despite the terror that was sweeping through her, she managed to keep the upper hand on both herself and the car and reached Gillybeck without further mishap.

The moment she got out of the car, the immediate danger over, she wondered what she'd gotten into a state about. It wasn't like her. She'd driven in snow before; in one instance she'd been caught in a blizzard that had been far worse than this and had not been flustered. At the same time, she was not foolhardy and knew that she'd better not waste time in doing what she had to do in case conditions worsened.

She couldn't find anything even remotely suitable to give Cliff as a present, but that was now no longer the main issue. Phoning Miles was.

She stepped into the telephone box, searched her purse for the necessary coins and dialed his number with the feeling of one who is going to the scaffold.

The monotonous brr-brrr, brr-brrr of the dial tone seemed to go on endlessly. She thought he must be out and was on the point of replacing the receiver when he answered. Miraculously, in those appalling conditions, his voice came strongly down a line that was clear of interference.

'Miles, it's me, Ros.'

'Ros! How marvelous. Happy Christmas.'

'Happy Christmas, Miles. I hope it's the best ever.' And I hope you take this stone from my heart. 'When I phoned last time, do you remember telling me about the man who was working with my father, the one who'd come home on sick leave who said he'd look me up if he got the chance?'

'Yes.'

110

'You tried to tell me something about him, but the line was so bad I couldn't make out what. Do you remember what it was?'

'Too well, I do. It's not something easily forgotten.'

The gravity of his tone struck fresh fear into Ros's heart.

'Wh-what was it?'

'While he was out there, he contracted an incurable illness.'

'Incurable?'

'Poor devil, he's come home to die. Your father said for me to be sure to tell you that there's no call for you to worry.'

'You've just told me he's going to die. And you say that!'

The note of hysteria in her voice received a concerned 'Are you all right, Ros?'

'Yes—yes, I'm all right.'

'Your father meant it in the sense that it's nothing you could catch. You know your trouble, don't you?'

'No, you tell me.'

'You've got too much feeling. You can't take everyone's grief on your shoulders. They aren't broad enough. So it's sad for the poor guy. But these things happen. Feel sympathy for him, by all means—it's tough luck to be cut down in the prime of life—but don't make it into a personal burden.'

'Does he . . . know?'

'Yes. I'm wishing you didn't. I had misgivings

111

about passing on that part of the message, but I respected your father's wish that you should know. I think he thought it would give you more understanding, make you think kindlier toward him. I don't suppose a man who's under the sentence of death feels like a bundle of fun.'

'No . . . I don't suppose so.'

'I didn't know you'd take it this bad.'

'How do you know how I'm taking it?'

'By your voice, what else? It's got a brittle quality that I don't like.'

'I'll be all right. You've just winded me, that's all. It's so dreadful . . . so . . .' She beat the panel where the coins were inserted with her free hand in a useless gesture of hitting back. Poor Cliff. How must he have felt when he found out? How must he be feeling now? 'I must go, Miles. It's snowing pretty heavily, and I've got to get back to the cottage. Good-bye. Don't worry about me. I'll be fine.'

Even in the crippling numbness of her despair, her brain was shrieking at her that she had to get back to Cliff. She couldn't bear it if she was snowed up there, away from him. She hadn't asked Miles if he knew how long Cliff had. She almost dialed his number again, then decided that she didn't want to know. She would spare herself that. The realization that their time together was limited was the worst blow that life had inflicted upon her. Losing her mother had been bad, but she had been

112

cushioned by her youth. She had been too young to understand the finality of death.

'I don't suppose a man who's under the sentence of death feels like a bundle of fun,' Miles had said. But Cliff had been a bundle of fun. His braveness astounded her. The fun they'd had snowballing one another that morning highlighted what attitude he'd decided to take. However much or little time that was left to him, he was going to enjoy it, and somehow she must follow that lead.

As she stumbled back to her car, she didn't feel the stabbing bite of the snow on her face, so much stronger was the pain that engulfed her heart as more memories tumbled into her awareness, his consideration for her being paramount. She understood his strange attitude toward her, the way he'd rushed her to begin with as if there wasn't a moment to lose, as indeed there wasn't. Then it was as if he'd stood back and taken stock, asked himself what that would do to her afterward. She'd let him know so plainly that before their relationship advanced another step, she wanted a more secure commitment, something lasting and binding. And all he could commit himself to was the moment. Oh, dear heaven, because now she remembered practically her last words to him on the subject. 'You aren't going to be a devastating thirty-two-year-old forever. Time could be running out for you.' She must have hurt him bitterly, and all he could think about was not hurting her. He'd told her so. 'You little fool, I'm trying my best not to hurt you,' he'd said.

Ros couldn't remember anything of the return journey. She went through the motions like an automaton, only realizing she was back at Holly Cottage when it occurred to her that the engine of the car wasn't throbbing anymore.

The door of the cottage was wrenched open, and Cliff's tall figure came looming toward her, the terrifying Heathcliff of childhood memory. He jerked the car door open and half dragged, half lifted her out. 'Are you all right? I should never have let you go off on your own in this. I didn't realize how bad it was. Why the hell didn't you turn back, you idiot child? I've been out of my mind with worry.'

His tone verged on anger, but she knew it was because of his concern for her, and that gave the pain in her heart another twist. He could think of her at a time like this, in spite of all he was going through.

'I'm sorry,' he said, 'I didn't mean to bark at you. It's just that . . .' He didn't attempt to qualify that remark but said instead, 'You don't need to look so stricken now. The nightmare's over. You're home.'

It was strange, nice, to be fussed over and cosseted, even though there was as much temper in his actions as tenderness; his reaction under the circumstances, she supposed. But

114

she should be cosseting him, she thought as his arm came supportively round her and he marched her into the cottage.

He helped her out of her coat and flung it over a chair with none of the fastidious care that was second nature to her when dealing with her clothes. The flakes of snow it had collected on its short journey from the car to the cottage began to melt and make puddles on the floor. If there was any wetness on her face, she hoped he would think it was the snow melting on her lashes and not the tears biting under her lids. He sat her down on the other kitchen chair, kneeling at her feet to remove her boots, which received the same rough treatment as her coat and were thrown into a corner. Even though it felt wrong for him to look after her, she knew it was right. Until she got herself together, it was better for him to think that she was trembling and in a state of shock because of the snowy conditions she had been caught up in, that she had felt terrified and unable to cope. She had to blame her lack of composure on something, and that excuse was as good as any and better than most. Whatever the temptation, she must not let on that she knew about him. She knew instinctively that he wouldn't want to share it with her but would rather she ignored it.

She felt chilled to the bone, as if she would never be warm again, but with her chair drawn up to the fire in the living room, her fingers clasped round the hot toddy that Cliff had prepared for her, standing over her and insisting that she drink it, she began to give an outward appearance of having thawed out.

He disappeared for a while, and when he returned, he said: 'I've put a hot water bottle in your bed. An early night wouldn't come amiss.'

She rose with the obedience of a child. 'You're right. I do feel rather exhausted. I'll go to bed.' She sent him a look of appeal. 'Don't I get a good-night kiss?'

He dropped one on the end of her nose, propelled her round and administered a slight push that directed her feet toward the stairs.

She went through the familiar routine of undressing, washing her face and cleaning her teeth, putting on her nightgown and brushing her hair. She heard Cliff come up the stairs. She caught her breath as his step hesitated outside her door and released it in a rush as she heard him move along the passage to his own room.

She covered her face with her hands. Cliff, oh, Cliff, *darling*. How could something as horrible as this happen to you? You don't deserve it. Or if it did have to happen, why couldn't we have met up again sooner?

The thought of his going out of her life, having only just come back into it, filled her heart with an unbearable sadness. The brave face he was putting on shamed her. She had always thought that she would be able to bear whatever misfortune life inflicted upon her with courage and dignity. But she hadn't envisaged anything like this. It was too cruel. Why did people—nations—waste time warring and quarreling? Didn't anyone realize how comparatively short the normal life-span was— and when that life-span was cut even shorter—

She was gulping back tears. His every look, his every mannerism, would be stamped indelibly on her brain, but she wouldn't have Cliff. Never to see that smile on his mouth again. She had hated its mocking arrogance; so many times she had wished it were within her power to erase it. Yet suddenly it seemed—this was crazy—endearing. And how many times had her fingertips cringed into the palms of her hands at the way his eyes glanced over her, taunting her, desiring her?

How could she profess to have a heart filled with compassion for him and not sate that desire? Was she going to wait until it was too late? She raised her eyes slowly. Looking at her determined face in the mirror, she knew that the answer forming in her mind was the right one. She would have to be very casual, even joking, in her approach. He wouldn't make the move toward her—he was too honorable—so she would have to go to him. She wished she looked more attractive for him. She should be wearing fragile lace adorned with tiny silk rosebuds and lovers' knots, not practical brushed nylon. But she had never gone in for that kind of nonsensical nightwear. She frowned at her reflection; then a tremulous smile fluttered across her mouth. She wouldn't go to him in brushed nylon! She twirled the offending garment over her head and tossed it aside; then her feet were creeping along the passage to Cliff's room.

'Cliff? May I come in?' she called out.

'No—don't you dare! I'm starkers!'

His voice seemed to be coming from somewhere near the door. Observing that no strip of light filtered from beneath it, she said, 'It's dark. But if you're that modest, get into bed.' Inspiration came to her aid. She knew just the right approach. 'I've brought your present.'

'Stick it under the tree like any other civilized being, and I'll get it in the morning. I have a golden rule that I never open my presents until Christmas morning.'

Her teeth were beginning to chatter, they probably would have done, anyway, because it was cold standing there, but she was shivering more from fright than anything. If she didn't go in before her nerve went, she'd find herself hastening back to her room.

She compressed her lips and took a deep breath. Her hand closed round the doorknob. 'That's one rule you're going to have to break.' She opened the door and entered the room, smiling despite everything as she heard him dive into bed. 'It isn't gift-wrapped. I'm sorry about that.' Her voice was shaky, and she was sorry about that, too.

'I don't know what fool game you're playing at, but it's obvious that I'm not going to get any peace until you've handed it over. So do so, and get out!' he yelled.

'It's me. I'm your present,' she said, sliding into bed beside him.

His hands shot out. 'Oh, no, you don't!' She knew that he meant to evict her, but then his fingers contacted her naked flesh. 'Rusty, what am I going to do with you?'

'You need me to tell you that?' she asked in pretend incredulity, somehow managing to suppress the sob in her throat.

Another groan. His hands came up to clamp her face, as if he couldn't trust them to be free. 'It's a very sweet thing you're doing, Rusty, but I can't. And before you start making fun of that, I don't mean can't, like not able to, I mean can't, not to you.'

'Why? Don't you find me desirable? Don't you want me?'

'I've wanted you from the moment I set eyes on the grown-up you, but I'm not going to take you. You're warm and beautiful.' She wasn't so sure about the beautiful, although it was nice to be told that she was. But she was warm now. The bedclothes were cold—he hadn't pampered himself with a hot-water bottle— but the combined body heat they were

119

generating made one unnecessary. 'I must care about you; otherwise, I wouldn't be talking this way now. I'd be accepting what you're offering and hardly believing my luck.'

'So why aren't you?'

'Because I can't marry you, and you're too special for anything else. Stick to your principles, and hold out for the guy who'll give you what you've a right to expect. Marriage and a settled future.'

It ripped her apart to hear him say that. He was pretending that he could marry her and give her a settled future if he'd wanted to. He was making it appear as though he were being selfish about this so that she'd go away. And it was just the reverse. She asked herself how anyone could be so *un*selfish. Anyone with a heart would forgive him for taking everything that she was offering. It was both touching and wonderful that he was willing to deny himself for her—putting her feelings before his own—and it increased her determination.

'Somehow, the things that mattered aren't all that important anymore. Who needs a silly old wedding certificate and the things that supposedly go with it!' she scoffed.

'Just who are you trying to convince? Me or yourself?'

'I'm being serious. I've been living in a child's dream. But now I've grown up.'

'It won't work, Rusty. My regard for you is too high for me to use you to satisfy my lust.

My lust for your innocence. You wouldn't be getting a good enough bargain.'

That was a debatable point. She knew that if she didn't give Cliff that comfort, she wouldn't be able to live with her own conscience afterward.

And so the glib falsehood, the lie by implication, fell from her lips. 'Really, Cliff! How unrealistic can you get? How innocent of you to think that I'm a virgin! Has it slipped your mind that I've been engaged to be married?'

'No, I haven't forgotten that.' His voice came out sounding amazingly stilted. 'I just thought—'

She could sense that he was frowning. Pursuing her victory, she said silkily, 'I'm human, too, you know. I wish you'd stop being virtuous, or whatever it is you're being, and consider *me*.'

'I think stupid might be the correct description. And, dammit, it's you I'm considering,' he growled.

'But not in the right way. Hasn't it occurred to you that I might be missing out?'

'I wish you wouldn't talk like that. It cheapens you.'

'I'm sorry you see it that way. A woman gets the same kind of torments as a man. Perhaps I think you're cheapening me by making me do all the chasing.' Realizing that she should follow that up, do something to back up the experience she claimed to have, she knuckled his cheek and then turned her hand to draw her fingers down his taut throat and along the muscled hardness of his chest.

He grabbed hold of her hand, pushing away in a manner to fend her off, and then, on a muffled groan of despair, he used the leverage to bring her close, lifting her arm to kiss the tender pulse beating erratically on the inside of her wrist before trailing fingers of fire down her arm and across her back as he gathered her to his chest.

'Ros . . . oh, Ros,' he murmured against her ear, and she knew that as she had discarded Heathcliff in favor of Cliff, he had said good-bye to that rusty-haired little girl he had been so ready to tease. She was Ros now, a warm, delicious woman whose nearness was a delight to him.

His lips scraped sensuously across her cheek, plucking at the corner of her mouth, inveigling its softness to part for his prolonged pleasure in a long and fulfilling kiss. His fingers moved up through the richness of her hair, searching out the tender hollows behind her ears and the one at the nape of her neck that sent erotic ripples of feeling down her spine. She hadn't known that such an innocent touch could give such passionate pleasure. Her own hands roved over his chest; the thick, dark, masculine growth of hair prickled her sensitized palms, which dragged up to caress his strong neck before clasping his dark head adoringly. She was too electrified by it all to be anything more than the passive partner. She was burning up with an unexpected intensity of feeling, and she needed a second to get her labored breathing on some kind of even keel.

She had come to his bed for reasons of the most pure and selfless nature, but her reward was the most tormenting delight she had ever known. A torment she never, never wanted to end. His fingers seemed to spend forever acquainting themselves with her back; there wasn't a bump in her spine, a muscle or hollow, he didn't know in the most intimate detail. The direction changed, and now his touch traced her rib cage. Her heart leaped as the exploration inched higher, gently curving to the underside of one breast before cupping its fullness. And then she was wriggling in joy as his strong thumb stroked sensuous circles round the rosy crescent.

His mouth poured liquid fire into hers. He kissed her until she was insensible, gliding mindlessly to unscaled heights of delirium. A wild, uncontrollable longing swept through her, a craving that consumed her in its molten beat. Her stomach muscles contracted so violently that the pain was as intense as a cramp. In a way, she supposed it was a kind of cramp, a sensual cramp, the driving anguish of her need. Her body was a hot aroused flame that wanted to wrap around him, yearned to be

123

absorbed by his strength.

His arm formed a tighter circle as he held her shuddering form more closely, but the appeasement she expected was denied her as his fingers lifted to stroke back the clinging damp tendrils of hair from her overheated brow.

'Are you absolutely sure, Ros?' he asked.

She had never been more sure of anything in her life. She had never sat down and defined her feelings for him, but if this emotion overflowing her heart wasn't love, she didn't know what love was. Being in love is wanting to give. She would have given her life for him; her body was such a small thing by comparison.

It wouldn't be true to say she was totally without inhibitions. There was still a hard core of apprehension and shyness deep within her that he hadn't touched, but that was getting easier to ignore all the time. It certainly wasn't solid enough for her to change her mind. She was ninety percent happy about things, smug, questioning how any woman could hold herself aloof from the man she loved. Love was the key for her. Love and unselfish devotion were above the niggardly ten percent of primness and principles. It seemed significantly less important that the affection was one-sided. He might not love her in the way she wanted him to love her, but he was loving in his actions. His patience with her was infinite, and she knew the rewards would be exceptional because of this, far exceeding the joys she'd experienced so far in his caring embrace. Her fingers gripped his shoulders on convulsive sweetness as her awakened body quivered on expectation.

'Yes, Cliff, I'm sure. So very, very sure.' When that did not unleash the primitive force of his passion, when he still made no move to possess her body, she said, 'Why do you ask?'

He took a long time in answering.

'I ask you because you are a liar, R—' His tongue stalled on the R that preceded her name, a momentary hesitation that made plain the nature of the lie he was accusing her of. He knew she was a virgin. If he goes back to calling me Rusty, I'll scream, she vowed—

'Ros,' he said, which was something at least.

'You know, don't you?'

'I'd have to be completely lacking in experience myself not to know that you are . . . untouched,' he finished delicately.

'Hardly untouched,' she said, finding his hand and tracing her fingertips across the tips of his.

'You know what I mean.'

'I still don't know why you stopped. You're acting as if my virginity is something to be prized which you mustn't violate.'

'It's special to you, Ros. For that reason, it's got to be special to the man who takes it.'

Her consolation was the tortured rawness of

125

his breath. He was denying himself, but not without great effort.

But he didn't have to. Even though his words had tapped on that doubting ten percent, she still had to help him, make it easy for him. It strengthened her resolve to do better.

Drawing in her breath, she said, 'Having got me to this pitch, you're not—not going to leave me unsatisfied, are you?'

'The answer to that should be a decisive yes, but I'm not that much of a saint, so let's talk it out some more. I don't want to leave either of us unsatisfied. I want you to understand that the score hasn't altered. Forgive me, but I've got to be brutal to be kind. Your sweetness isn't going to enslave my heart, if that's what you're thinking. I intend to remain free and uncommitted. If you're looking for a permanent relationship, you're in the wrong bed. I'm not sure how long I'll be hanging around. I've accumulated a fair bit of leave, so I can be flexible in my plans. But sooner or later, I'll up and go. You've got to understand that.'

She swallowed. How could he still pretend? How could he talk of going so rationally?

'Good grief! You're not crying, are you? I thought you were the girl who went for blunt speaking?'

'I am. Where are you going now?' she asked as the bed suddenly lightened.

'To get a handkerchief for you. I can't abide a soggy pillow.'

'To know that, you must have had experience of a soggy pillow. It wouldn't be your tears; you're too hard. I must assume that I'm not the first girl in your bed you've made cry.'

That snappy note was good. If she went soft on him, he might suspect that she knew about him. She sensed that he was already sifting about in his mind for her motive in coming to his bed. He was too quick by far. She mustn't let him know why she was there.

His face towered above hers again. She could just make out the shadowy outline of it and the bulk of his strong shoulders. She was glad it was dark, glad he couldn't see the quaking vulnerability in her eyes.

'I'm trying to do the right thing, Ros. It's not easy, believe me, but I've got to give you time to know that it is really what you want.'

'I've said it is, haven't I?'

'It's not enough to want it now. You've got to be happy about it in the morning.'

'I will be.'

'Perhaps I'm not just thinking of you. I want to be happy with it, as well. Something doesn't add up. There's got to be a reason behind this crazy impulse of yours. I want to know what it is.'

She sniffed, not trusting herself to speak.

'Here.' The handkerchief he'd gone to fetch

127

was pushed into her hand. His fingers brushed the top of her head. 'Get some sleep, Ros. We'll talk again in the morning.'

'Aren't you—?'

'No. Don't disturb yourself. I'll take your bed. I must be going soft in the head,' she heard him say as he moved away.

## CHAPTER SEVEN

Sleep was a long time in coming, so not surprisingly, she woke to the realization that it was two hours later than her normal waking time. On Christmas day, too, with so much to do! Even then she knew that it was an alien presence entering her room that had disturbed her. Looking round, she saw that it wasn't her room but Cliff's, and the alien presence was none other than the man himself bearing a breakfast tray.

'What a rare treat,' she said, sitting up forgetfully and then, on seeing what Cliff saw, reaching hastily for the pajama jacket he'd put out in readiness the night before but had not got round to wearing.

His expression told her that it was prudish to be that modest after what had occurred between them, and what had almost occurred, the previous night. Even though part of her mind did agree with him, she did the buttons.

128

Perhaps it was this step back into strait-laced virtue that made up Cliff's mind to tease. The gleam in his eyes was in close pursuit of the smile tugging up his mouth as he said, 'I always give breakfast in bed to females who come into my room at dead of night to have their way with me.'

She pulled a face at him. 'But I didn't.'

'No,' he said sorrowfully.

'Don't tell me you're regretting running out on me?'

'What do you think? I regret it like hell, but I would have regretted it more if I'd stayed.'

With her breath suspended in her lungs, Ros said, 'That's stupid. I came to you last night with my eyes open and my qualms squashed. In other words, I'm admitting that you are right and I've been sadly wrong. One should grab happiness as and when one can.'

He frowned. 'That's a dangerous viewpoint to take.' He plonked the tray down on her knee.

Catching hold of it with a steadying hand, she noticed that the egg and two rashers of bacon were beautifully cooked, the toast done to a golden turn. 'It's your viewpoint,' she defended.

'I'm a man.'

Her eyes slid mischievously up to his face. 'I had noticed.'

That furrowed his frown deeper. 'Men aren't as vulnerable to hurt as women are.'

'Could it be that you're changing your tune?'

'No. So don't go building up your hopes. I'd be bored with the same woman. Variety has always been the spice of affection for me.'

'Don't you think your affections are capable of being constant to one woman?' she asked, just as if there were a point in pursuing the issue.

'No, for the simple reason that people aren't constant. They change. It isn't in the course of nature to stay the same, or we'd all be trapped forever in childhood. And that's a horrifying thought to dwell on. Take you, for example, you're not the same girl you were yesterday. You're not thinking the same. As the years progress, you'll change even more. In, say, five years' time, you'll have altered so much as to be hardly recognizable as the girl you are now. The chances are that the changes may not be to my fancy. It's unfair to ask any man to pledge his life to someone he may not even like before the first decade is out.'

'I couldn't agree more about the horror of remaining static in childhood. That's one change for the better, so why can't the others be, as well? People mature physically and mentally, but feelings remain the same. Only a cynic or a very shallow person would think otherwise.'

'Take your pick. Which am I, a cynic or shallow?'

130

'A cynic. You believe deeply in what you believe, even though your beliefs are misguided.'

She shook her head on the futility of going on, taking an extremely long time over cutting a piece of bacon and piercing it with her fork but delaying transferring it to her mouth, needing the pretext to keep her eyes lowered. Of course, Cliff was cynical. He'd every right to be considering the blow he'd been delivered, and she was close to tears, frustrated that she could do nothing to rescind his fate and angry with herself for wasting one precious moment fighting with him.

'In every way, Ros,' his voice boomed out over her bowed head, 'I'm glad you're not with my beliefs. They're fine for me, but I don't want you to absorb them. It's all right for a man to play the field, but a woman needs constancy. There's a name for a woman who indulges in casual affairs.'

There was a name for a man who took that chauvinistic viewpoint—and a question burning in her brain. If all women remained constant, where were all the free-loving men going to find their excess of loose women? She could have pointed out the unrealism attached to his way of thinking except that she'd made up her mind not to argue with him, so she said sweetly, 'If you say so, Cliff.'

That didn't suit him, either. Sending her a dark and suspicious look, he inquired: 'You

131

wouldn't be taking the micky out of me, would you?'

'That wasn't my intention. I merely sought an end to the discussion so that I could eat my breakfast in peace.'

'Are you saying that I'm so unreasonable that the only way to shut me up is to agree with me?'

'No-o,' she said on a long, quivering sigh of exasperation. 'I have a million and one things to do. Top priority is getting the turkey into the oven.'

He leaned forward and fiddled with the top button of her borrowed pajama jacket. 'That's not my top priority. Can't we open a couple of cans?'

Slapping his fingers away, imperiling the tray on her knee, she said, 'On Christmas day? Certainly not. Watch it! You'll have coffee all over your bed.'

'Then we'd have to transfer to your bed, wouldn't we?'

She knew that he didn't mean it, that he was only teasing her, calling her bluff. Just the same, she snapped: 'The only place I'm transferring to is the kitchen.'

'That doesn't sound like the bold female who came to my room last night.'

'You kicked her back into line.'

'Seems to me she can't have been all that determined, to be so easily deterred. I've never seen such a quick change of mind.'

'Who's had a change of mind? It wasn't a romantic impulse. I meant it. It's different, somehow, in the cold light of day. The atmosphere isn't the same, and it doesn't have the right mood.'

But wasn't she lying to herself? The mood wasn't dependent on the time or place but the people. Paradise wouldn't be paradise without the right companion, and Cliff's presence anyplace she happened to be would charge the air with electricity and give life's breath its extra sparkle. She was exhilarated by his closeness, and incalculably, insanely, in love with him, and in turn this made her feel—more than a little foolish. She was too vulnerable. She felt shy and self-conscious. A palpitating thrill ran through her as his eyes made a slow examination of her face, adding to her nervous tension and making her feel more at a disadvantage and more confused than ever.

It had taken a great deal of courage to do what she'd done the previous night. It might be cowardly of her, but she'd only been able to do it under cover of darkness. It wasn't in her nature to be blatant about it, and neither could she tell him why she'd done what she did. It was bad enough that Cliff knew how limited his future was; he would hate it if he thought she knew. He would be hurt and humiliated if he suspected that she'd offered herself to him out of compassion. Pity, however charitably extended, is invariably unwelcome, and to Cliff

133

it would be especially abhorrent because he had more pride than most men. The only way to go to him was to let him think she found him irresistible, as she did, and that he'd swept her off her feet—as he had just by looking at her.

Thinking about the bleakness of his future had undermined her. She felt perilously close to tears again. She mustn't let him see her distress. She couldn't explain it to him. She'd already made up her mind to follow his example and enjoy, yes, *enjoy*, the time they had, filling each day to full capacity with fun as if—as if it were the last . . .

Hiding the lost look of sadness and resignation in her eyes by lowering her lids and pretending absorption in the food before her, she said testily, 'What are you still hanging about for? I would have thought you'd better things to do.'

He grinned, helping himself to a piece of toast before doing as she asked by vacating the room and letting her finish her breakfast and get dressed. She was halfway through that when she remembered the two presents with her name on them under the tree. Her impatience to open them hurried her along, and so instead of pinning her hair back, she contained its looseness in a broad hair band that was in keeping with her wide-eyed childish eagerness. The turkey would have to wait a while longer before being popped into the oven.

One of the presents was in the shape of a flat, hard oblong, like a book. The other was bulkier and squashy to the touch, decorated with a lavish red and silver bow. She knelt on the floor, examining them, with Cliff indulgently looking on.

Tearing at the Christmas paper of the first one, saving the more intriguingly shaped package till last, she said: 'Getting presents is such fun. Especially when they're so excitingly wrapped.'

A wicked smile came to his lips. 'I thought it was fun, too, but for a different reason. I liked my present because it was excitingly unwrapped.'

Her fingers stilled on the paper. She looked up at him, a shy blush creeping to her cheeks. 'You rejected it.'

'Fool me.'

'I don't suppose I would have lived up to your other women, anyway,' she said ingenuously.

One black eyebrow arched at her. 'I could answer that in two ways. I could say, if you're that interested to know, there is a way of finding out. Then again, I could say, you might be inexperienced, but you showed fantastic potential.'

'Oh, yeah!' she mocked to cover her embarrassment.

'Don't draw comparisons, Ros. It could have

been wonderful, and I'll tell you why. Because you were, are, uniquely you. I'm sorry you weren't luckier.'

'Luckier?'

'In the fairy-tale, the princess kissed the frog, and he turned into a prince. I'm not likely to turn into your prince. I'm a frog through and through. Keep that in mind, and you won't be hurt.'

Nothing he could say would make her despise him or alleviate the bitter hurt that she knew would be hers. She hadn't known that her feelings would be this involved, that she would give so much of herself. Her lashes descended hastily, hiding her eyes. She must do better than this, and she could make a start by concentrating on his feelings and disregarding her own. Instead of going tearful on him every time she thought about the terrible thing that faced him and acting as if her virginity were sacrosanct and not to be infringed upon, she could make light of it so that he wouldn't feel guilty if . . . *when*, she amended hastily in her mind, it happened. She knew with staunch conviction that it would happen between them—they would make love. He might resist or she might resist in the confusing pendulum swing of emotions, but the outcome was inevitable.

Lifting her face, she said, 'Princes don't come wearing badges stating, "I'm a prince." And ordinary girls seem to lack the discernment of a fairy-tale princess, so I'll have to take my luck along with the rest.'

She pulled at the last bit of wrapping paper, and then her laughter was real. It was a book. 'Just what I've always wanted,' she said, gulping on hilarity. 'A cookery book.' At least it wasn't one that she had written.

His smile was slow in coming. Something had not amused him. Perhaps because he didn't know she was herself a cookery expert and writer of cookbooks, he thought she was laughing at him. Unless his mind was still lingering on the serious undertones of the frivolous conversation they'd just had about frogs and princes.

Eventually, the corners of his mouth struggled out of whatever grimness of thought had been clamping them in such black gloom, and she turned to the other gift. Both useful and adorable, it was a housecoat in midnight blue velvet with a tiny quilted collar and a quilted pocket motif.

She reached up to kiss his cheek. 'Thank you for my presents. I love them.' Her eyes said, 'I love you.' She never meant to send him that melting look. It had just happened. She regretted it instantly. Perhaps he hadn't read the message. But she knew that he had and had found it not to his liking.

He took her face in his hands, and his lips swooped in angry assault, as if endeavoring to bully the loving thoughts from her head, to stamp the moment with passion and punish her for daring to add a sweeter dimension.

He didn't so much release her as push her away, and the corners of her mouth turned down at the brutality. She occupied herself by scooping up the velvet housecoat. 'Just the thing to slip on at the tail end of an evening,' she said huskily. But the evening was a long way away; first there was a lovely day to *enjoy*, just as she'd determined, and damn his gloom!

His bad mood didn't last. They both took a share of the chores; busily, harmoniously, they worked side by side. A perfect twosome, Ros thought, now that good humor was restored between them. A robin perched on the windowsill, looking for crumbs, which were quickly taken out to him. At last, everything was ready. Ros changed into the red dress she had bought, and then they sat down to the special meal. They pulled crackers and wore the fancy hats that came out of them and laughed at the corny cracker jokes that they read out loud to each other. One joke slip was howlingly appropriate to a recently explored theme. Beneath a particularly revolting drawing of a frog gloating over a pretty girl, the caption read, 'It's a girl's lot to kiss a lot of frogs in her search for her prince.' It wasn't that much of a coincidence, because the cracker selection was called *One Day My Prince Will Come.* The box had been under the tree, and doubtless Cliff's eyes had lit upon it as they'd talked, and it had prompted his observation in the first place, but it was so screamingly funny that Ros fell about laughing, and she put the slip of paper on one side to save.

Day slid into evening. They drew the curtains, shutting out the cold, frosty, fairy-tale world. They didn't have a sophisticated stereo deck, just a small transistor radio, but it provided music to dance to. Ros had been sitting on the sofa, her slippers kicked off and her feet tucked under her, when Cliff proffered the invitation. Because she danced barefoot, her head didn't ascend to the curve of his neck as it had before, and he had to bend his head a long way to kiss her. He seemed to take a long time in deciding whether he wanted to kiss her or not—and then it was as if the decision were taken out of his hands. The compulsion to do so wouldn't be fended off a moment longer.

The night before, she'd been positive that her lips had known every delight there was, but this deeply explorative kiss swept open new doors and took her down into endless depths of pleasure. She felt as though she were drowning in sensualism, and she never wanted to surface. When she did, it wasn't long before he reclaimed her lips, and the dizzy delight dragged her back down into the bliss again. Her arms went up round his neck. Her head was driven back as the kiss deepened; her concave spine brought her body closer still to his. His hand on the small of her back burned through her dress and fused them together for a brief, deciding moment, and then he reached up and untangled her fingers.

'Time to put on your housecoat,' he instructed, starting off a slow, sweet explosion of feeling in her stomach. 'I'll make us a bedtime drink.'

Ros went upstairs, undressed and reached for her housecoat. Without stopping to deliberate, she knew that it was the only garment she would put on. The soft touch of velvet felt good against her skin. When she came back down, she looked for the joke slip about the girl kissing a lot of frogs before she found her prince, but she couldn't find it. It must have got cleared away with the rest of the debris. It didn't matter.

Cliff appeared carrying two mugs of hot chocolate. They drank it in drowsy content, their eyes meeting in question . . . answer . . . and then anticipation.

As he put out a hand to assist her to her feet, the tingling awareness that his kisses had aroused vibrated in her fingertips. They went up the stairs, down the passage to the cozy end room.

The housecoat she had just put on, Cliff proceeded to take off. Sliding the first button free, he said, 'You're right. Unwrapping a present is exciting fun, but it isn't the best

140

part.'

That had been a joking statement, a quip of the moment best forgotten. She wished he'd stop harping on about it. It made her feel cheap. Because he didn't suspect that she knew what she did, he couldn't know what had motivated her. He probably thought she was hot for him. But she wanted him to think that she had no deeper motivation than that so that he would neither feel humiliated by her unacceptable compassion nor guilty for his selfishness in taking what she was so selflessly giving? Of course she did. But she also wanted him to think well of her. She couldn't have it all ways. It wouldn't make her feel good if she made him feel bad.

'I didn't say it was the best part, Cliff.'

'No, you didn't.'

A pulse fluttered in her throat as he dealt with the second button.

'What's the matter?' he asked.

Had she tensed away? 'Nothing.'

Neither of them had bothered to shut the curtains, and a pale moon glanced in at the window. As the third button was undone, Cliff's smoldering eyes ran down her throat, the white gleam of her collarbone, to the beauty of her breasts, which cast moon shadows on his hands as he undid the fourth button, exposing her skin to the fragile, silvery glimmer.

As he lifted his face, the soft light carved his

strong features into strange planes and thrust his eyes into deep, unreadable hollows. There was a harshness about the silver-sheened mask. His voice matched the hardness of his mouth but quivered with the same passion of feeling that she sensed she would have read in his eyes if their expression hadn't been hidden from her. 'You look like a moon goddess, a strange, ethereal maiden from another planet. Will you be spirited away if I touch you?'

'Why don't you . . . find out for yourself?' she invited in a choked, hushed voice.

He put a hand on either side of her face. 'So far so good. So *good*,' he repeated, his voice little more than a guttural groan as he proceeded to kiss her on the mouth. His hands transferred to her throat and eased the housecoat from her shoulders. The velvet material sighed softly past her hips. He looked at her for a long moment; then she was lost, clinging to him as he carried her to the bed.

His hands and mouth adored her face, her throat, her shoulders, her breasts, before leaving her for a moment to quiver in expectancy, returning to slide his naked body against hers. Her arms curved round his neck, her hands followed the thick muscled cords and dug into his hair as she pressed her awakened body closer to his.

He was so vital, so alive. He made *her* feel vital and alive. How could he be going to die? How could he accept it so calmly? Be so brave? She wished she were braver. Oh, dear Lord, she was going to cry again. She *was* crying. Tears filled her eyes; hopelessly, helplessly, they fell down her cheeks.

'I'm sorry, Cliff.'

'Sorry!' he spluttered.

'I'm not brave like you.' Oh, dear, she must be careful what she said.

'Brave? What are you talking about? You don't get awards of gallantry for this pastime.'

And still he could joke!

Her admiration for him knew no bounds as she said, 'Take no notice of me. I'm being silly. It's nothing.'

'Nothing! One moment you're a woman inviting me to make love to you, and the next you're blubbering like a child because I am. I wish you'd make up your mind what you want.'

'I have. I know what I want.'

She kept her chin tucked into her neck. She dared not look at him. A few moments ago, the moon sliding in on them had seemed beautifully romantic; now she wished it would hide its face behind a cloud so that she couldn't see Cliff's face. She didn't want to see what his expression revealed. It wasn't the anger she knew would be in his eyes that she cringed from but the contempt. What must he think of her? Whatever it was, it was no worse than what she thought of herself.

'Do you?' he asked, his fury held on a very short rein. 'I disagree. You're about as mixed up as anyone can be, and you're mixing me up, too. I'd be fully justified in showing you that you're not getting away with this. The frustrating part of it is, I don't know what it is you're doing, even though I know all too well what it's doing to me. The old brain box is telling me this is a deliberate and subtle play upon my emotions. On the other hand, my reason is overruling the cynic in me and stressing emphatically that you're not consciously cold and calculating but warm and impulsive. Do me a favor, curb those impulses until you can follow through. There isn't a man on earth who could stand this sort of treatment.'

'Cliff . . . please . . . don't go.'

'Be reasonable, Ros. Would there be any point in my staying?'

'I don't know.'

But as she watched him walk away, she made no attempt to call him back again, because she knew that he was right. They couldn't get together until she got herself together. It was no good having noble thoughts and no backbone.

\* \* \*

It stopped snowing on Boxing Day and a steady thaw set in. The roads were slushy but passable. The mood between them was still slightly frosty, but not bad, all things

144

considered. She couldn't quibble if Cliff was short-tempered with her, because she felt that it was her fault. She knew she was going to have to pare off some of the precious time they had together to come to terms with the situation. She had to get herself in hand so that she could be a comfort to him, not the irritation and source of anger and annoyance she was. The clear roads would serve a double purpose. She could get to the New Year's Day book-signing session she had promised to do and perhaps sort herself out at the same time.

On telling Cliff that business called her back to town, he asked, 'What business?'

'It's to do with my writing.'

'Oh—the book you're on with? How to catch your man?' he said, referring to the theme she had mentioned when first telling him about it.

'Mm.' She had regained her confidence on the cooking front and could now own to the truth. 'Through his stomach. It's a cookbook. But my business isn't to do with that book; it's the one before it. I'm doing a book-signing session.'

'On the same subject, I take it, if I read that gloating smile right. Yes? Well, in all fairness, I must admit that you'd be an extremely good cook if your concentration didn't wander.' She glared at him because they both knew that he was responsible for that but made no comment. He continued, 'It's getting so that I'm not surprised at anything you do.' His

145

frown could have meant that some of the surprises were not to his liking or indicated displeasure that she was going away. 'How long will you be gone?'

'I think I should plan on two nights. I'll leave here on New Year's Eve day and return on the second of January.' It was uplifting to know that he expected her to come back.

*     *     *

It was a long journey. Normally, she liked driving, but the fact that she was driving away from Cliff robbed her of the pleasure of being behind the wheel. Yet when she arrived, making straight for the house where Miles and his sister Hannah lived, a glow of happiness shot through her at seeing her agent and very good friend again. Her *two* good friends, because she had always got on well with Hannah in spite of frequently bridling at the older woman's bossy and managing manner.

Taking both her hands and pressing them to his lips, Miles said, 'Good to see you, Ros. How are you?'

'I'm fine. How are you?'

'Making it do.'

'Rosalynd, my dear.' Hannah was the only person who called her by her full name. 'How are you *really*?' She wasn't as easily taken in as her brother, and there was speculation in the shrewd blue eyes.

146

Miles saved her from answering by asking, 'Where are you staying?'

Had she told him she'd given up her flat? She didn't think so. But obviously he'd heard. Just how much had he heard? she wondered. Did he know about Jarvis and Glenis?

This time she was forestalled by Hannah. 'She's staying with us, of course, Miles. Where else did you think? Go and garage Rosalynd's car, and bring in her suitcase.'

Ros sighed. She wondered how she was going to get it across to Hannah that she was all right and that she didn't want to be tucked under her wing.

Miles didn't look to Ros to see if that arrangement was suitable to her and sealed Ros's immediate fate by obeying his sister's command. Hannah had a quiet authority about her that usually got her her own way, and if Ros were truthful, she would be more comfortable there than booking into a hotel as she had planned. Moreover, she realized how ungrateful she was being by her lack of response. She knew that Hannah's warm generosity in wanting her should be rewarded with a smile.

Her mouth curved dutifully. 'Thank you, Hannah. That's very kind of you.'

She didn't doubt that it was well meant, but Ros found Hannah's concern far from comforting, much preferring Miles's hoodwinked and blinkered attitude. It would

147

have pleased her if Hannah had been equally unobservant and not seen the sorrow hiding behind her smile. However, Hannah didn't use Miles's absence to pump her, although Ros knew she wasn't getting off this lightly and that it would come later.

Hannah took her up to the pretty guest room. Because it was south facing, getting whatever sunshine was going, the color scheme was predominantly blue and white. Blue carpet flecked with white. Blue and white patterned wallpaper, with warm splashes of color in the pink bedspread and the pink, hand-crocheted mats on the dressing table and chest of drawers.

'These are beautiful,' Ros said, touching one. 'One of these days I'm going to learn to crochet.'

'Really!' Hannah drawled in amusement. 'A little old lady does them for me.'

Ros hadn't thought for a moment that she was admiring Hannah's handiwork. Hannah was a tall, cool blonde. Ros knew that she was slightly older than Miles, which would put her in her early forties, but she didn't look it. Ros had once said to Miles that she couldn't understand why Hannah had never married. Miles had confided with a dry shaft of humor that it was his opinion that his sister had never found a man she wanted to boss sufficiently enough to marry him.

'I think you'll be comfortable here,' Hannah

said.

'I'm sure I will be. It's a lovely room, a tribute to your exquisite taste.'

'Thank you. I hope you don't mind my saying this.'

Ros's heart plummeted. When someone prefaced a sentence with that, it was usually something you did mind.

'. . . even though I don't know the reason for your breakup with Jarvis, I want you to know that I'm backing your judgment. I think you did the right thing in walking out on him, and you'll be doing the wrong thing if you go back to him.'

Ros's spirits lifted. She didn't mind talking about Jarvis. There was no hurt there anymore. She'd thought that Hannah wanted to pry out of her what had happened in Yorkshire, and she wanted to keep Cliff to herself. It was too special and private to be subjected to even the kindest curiosity. Moreover, though she might hate Hannah's overbearing interference, she knew it was motivated by the best of intentions. A heart of pure gold beat behind the plastic facade that Hannah put on. Ros had nothing to back that notion, but she thought that Hannah deliberately erected that protective shell round herself. She put on a 'How quaint!' look and pretended to scoff at homely things, like, for example, hand-crocheted mats, so that no one could know the real Hannah. Had someone—a

man—gotten too close to Hannah, and had she
been hurt?

'I haven't much faith in men as a species,
except for Miles, of course, and Jarvis is a
pretty odious specimen,' Hannah said.

Oh, yes, Ros was certain that she was on the
right track.

'Naturally, he's giving it out that the
engagement was broken off by mutual
consent.'

'And you don't believe him?' Ros said. 'You
are right. But perhaps face-saving untruth is
better than nasty mud raking.'

'How nasty? Very? Or only a little?'

'Only a little. I came upon him with another
girl.' Past loyalty made Ros withhold Glenis's
name, because Hannah wouldn't think much
of a girl who took advantage of her
roommate's absence to make up to her fiancé.

'Does it still hurt?'

'No. I've since realized that I didn't care
enough for Jarvis.'

'In other words, you've had a lucky escape?
I'm glad about that. I'm fond of you, Rosalynd,
and so I've been worried about you. Guilty,
too, I suppose, because you met Jarvis here.'

'Yes, I did. Fancy you remembering that.'

'It's kind of you not to blame us for that
disastrous introduction. Apparently you
don't?'

'Of course not.'

'In Miles's profession, he has to appear

friendly on the surface with people he wouldn't otherwise tolerate. Acting as his hostess, I have to back him to the hilt.'

'I understand.'

'No, you don't, not yet. I haven't told you everything. There's something that momentarily slipped my mind when I invited you to stay with us. We're having a party tomorrow evening. As you know, we always have a New Year's Day party. That way we get everybody, because most people have their parties on New Year's Eve.'

'Yes. So?'

'Jarvis is on the guest list.'

'You want me to make myself scarce?'

'Heaven forbid! I want you there. You're always a useful extra pair of hands. I didn't know how you'd feel about coming face to face with him again, that's all.'

'I don't feel a thing either way. So stop fussing.'

'It's a brave girl who tells my sister to stop fussing,' Miles announced at the door. 'One suitcase,' he said, coming in and setting it down. 'I hope there's a pretty dress in there.'

'There is,' Ros assured him.

'I was just telling Rosalynd about the party tomorrow evening,' Hannah said.

'Ros doesn't need telling about that. It's a ritual. The new year couldn't start without our party. I was thinking of the one we're going to this evening at the Searle's and wondering if

151

Ros might care to gate crash.'

'M'mm . . . yes! Better than that. I'll give Naomi Searle a ring and ask if we may bring Rosalynd.'

'No,' Ros said, feeling that it was time she stood up to Hannah. 'I'd much prefer to stay here.'

There was a limit to how far one could be swept along, but that wasn't her sole reason for her determination not to go with them to the party. Only just parted, and she was missing Cliff terribly. She didn't want to put on a social face and say all the right things to all the wrong people. She wanted to be by herself and think of Cliff.

## CHAPTER EIGHT

The next day, Miles suggested she leave her car in the garage and offered to drive her to the place where the book-signing session was going to be held. He delivered her, coming in and staying long enough to have a word or two with people he knew, and said he'd return for her later to take her home.

It was a good day. Time passed quickly, and she couldn't believe it when Miles came back for her.

'Ready?'

'As soon as I collect my coat.'

She returned to the table she'd been using to find Miles in conversation with a man. At first, she thought he was a latecomer wanting a book autographed, but he turned to her in the manner of someone who knew her.

'I was just inquiring after you, Miss Seymour,' he said. 'I saw the ad in the newspaper about today, but I couldn't get here any sooner, and I thought I must have missed you.'

He was of average height with a shock of gray hair and the weathered skin of someone who has spent much of his life out-of-doors. She wasn't too good on ages, but she gauged him to be about twenty years her senior. She couldn't remember ever having met him before, but obviously she must have. That he was talking to Miles auto-suggested to her that it must have been at Miles's house. Miles and Hannah entertained a lot, and it was difficult to keep track of all the people she'd met there.

'If you'd been any later, you would have missed me, Mr.—'

'Edward.' He cut in so swiftly that she was saved the embarrassment of floundering. 'Mr. Banks sounds so formal.'

Thank you, Mr. Banks. Edward Banks. The name meant as little to her as his face did.

There was a tension about Miles. He looked as uncomfortable as a man whose shoes are too tight for him. Had he had an argument with Edward Banks at some time? But then

153

Miles killed this thought of hers by turning to the other man, a broad, genuine smile on his face.

'My sister and I are throwing a party tonight, Edward. Why don't you come along?'

'Thank you, yes. I'd love to.'

Miles took a small printed card from his pocket. 'In that case, you'll need the address.'

Ros didn't think anything strange in this. Miles had moved house about eight months before, so it was probable for someone who had temporarily dropped out of the social scene not to know where he lived.

The three of them chatted for a while longer. Ros wished she could bring Edward Banks back to memory. It would have helped the conversation along. She was surprised that her mind was such a blank. It wasn't as if he was an insignificant little man, easily forgotten; he had a forceful, likable personality.

On the way back to Miles's house, she considered asking Miles about him. She said nothing, bowing to ego—she didn't want to admit to Miles that she was slipping. Perhaps when she met Edward Banks later at the party, something might click.

Miles and Hannah's parties were always swish affairs. Ros, knowing about the New Year's Day ritual and anticipating an invitation, had packed accordingly, selecting the lovely ice-blue gown she had rejected in favor of the more sensuous green when Cliff had wined and dined her just before Christmas. The bright color of her hair struck a note of contrast to the cool elegance of the dress. She decided to wear her hair down, the way Cliff liked it. Would Cliff always dictate her thoughts, even after—? No, she mustn't think about that. She must look optimistically to the future. She couldn't believe that Cliff was going to die. Medical science had made enormous strides, different methods of treatment were tried, new miracle drugs were being discovered all the time.

Her door opened after a peremptory warning tap, and Hannah walked in looking very sophisticated in black, a color she tended to favor; and it did enhance her blond beauty. She smelled expensively of Bal à Versailles.

Ros hoped that Hannah would read the extra brightness in her eyes—that thoughts of Cliff had brought—as party excitement.

'Rosalynd, how lovely you look.'

'So do you, Hannah. But then you always do look gorgeous.'

They went down together. On these occasions, Ros was inevitably roped in to do the food. But as she hadn't been on hand, a firm of caterers had been hired. Everything was in order, looking appetizing and decorative on a long buffet table. The sofas and chairs had been pushed against the walls to give more center space for circulating and for a carpet shuffle should anyone get the urge to dance to

155

the background stereo music. The ringing of the doorbell heralded the arrival of the first lot of guests.

To begin with, people arrived in a trickle, but then everyone seemed to come at once, and the party was in full swing. It wasn't long before Jarvis came to find her. She had buckled in straightaway, taking round a tray of food, and had stayed chatting with the group that had relieved her of the remaining cocktail snacks. Jarvis took the empty tray from her hand, reared it against the wall, hooked his arm through hers and walked her away to a relatively quiet corner. 'Where we can talk,' he said.

Ros felt there was nothing to talk to Jarvis about, but one or two speculative eyebrows had risen at his approach and subsequent conduct. To make a fuss would have been to refute the 'parting by mutual consent' propaganda Jarvis had put around.

'You're looking exceptionally attractive this evening, Ros,' he said.

'And you are looking your usual debonair self. But really, Jarvis,' she said, her party smile firmly in place, 'is there any purpose in this?'

'What's the harm in saying hello to an old friend?'

'Hello, old friend. Now I really must help Hannah, so if you'll excuse me—'

'Running out on me? That's not very

156

cordial. I see I shall have to take you in hand again.'

'I'm flattered that you should want to, but no.'

'You can't cancel out what we had so easily, Ros.'

'Can't I? You did!'

Choosing to ignore that barb, he said, 'That damned cottage was at the root of our troubles. You thought more about it than you did of me. All that nostalgic wallowing into your childhood was unhealthy. You should have been concentrating on the future, our future together.'

'We haven't got one, Jarvis. I'm sorry.'

'You can't mean that. When you went away, you led me to believe there was a chance that we'd get back together.'

'But later I said that you should consider yourself free. I had to get away to think things over, but I didn't tie you down to a possibility that might never happen. I think I knew then that it was over between us.'

'I want you back, Ros.'

'It's no good, Jarvis. Anyway, what about Glenis?'

'We rowed. We aren't talking now. So you see, you don't have anything to worry about in that direction. I've learned my lesson. I'll behave myself if you'll give me another chance.' His lower lip jutted out in the manner of a small chastened boy. In the old days, it

157

had never failed to bring a smile to her mouth, but it did nothing at all for her now.

'I'm sorry things didn't work out for you and Glenis, because I think you were made for each other.' She could have said *deserved each other.* Had he gotten the inflection, or had he been on the verge of turning nasty anyway?

'Have you met someone else?' he asked sourly.

'Yes,' she admitted.

'That didn't take long.' Two couples were taking advantage of a record that was being played and shuffling in time to the music. Jarvis wasn't so lacking in perception that he didn't know she was on the point of walking away from him. 'Dance?' he said, a sneer on his handsome mouth as his arm went round her waist, effectively trapping her.

'I don't want to dance with you.'

'I suppose you'd rather be dancing with him?' he said, his fingers digging cruelly deep into her flesh.

'Yes. Too true I would!'

'Is it Miles? I always did think his attitude was a bit too fond. And it won't have taken him long to figure out that there's more glory in being your husband than your agent. And, after all, he did land the contract for you.'

'What are you talking about?'

'Celebrities aren't usually so modest. The slot you're doing for television, what else? Miles thinks you're going somewhere. Can't blame the guy for making sure he holds on to you.'

'Is that why you wanted me?' she gasped.

'No, of course not!' The vehement denial would have had more backing if he'd been able to meet her eyes and if its cutting edge hadn't been dulled by embarrassment. 'We were friendly before the television company approached you.'

'Friendly before, yes! But you didn't propose to me until afterward! I've been a bigger fool than I thought,' she said, dignity masking her dismay. 'It isn't any of your business, but it isn't Miles. His attitude toward me is that of a good friend, which is what he is. Now, will you please release me.'

Instead of doing as she asked, he tightened his arm around her. It was strange to feel revulsion at close physical contact with a man she had been on the brink of marrying. If they had married, she would have had to submit to more than this unwelcome public fondling, and she realized that she'd had an even luckier escape than she'd thought. Repugnance stiffened her body as his hand slid lower than her waist, and that adverse response made Jarvis angrier still.

'Loosen up, you might enjoy it.'

'I'll enjoy kicking you on the shins if you don't stop this.'

'Why should I?' It must have occurred to Jarvis that he'd burned his boats and had nothing more to lose. 'You've got the kind of body a man likes to warm his hands on. Has he warmed his hands on you yet, Ros? The color of your hair sets my senses on fire—but all there is underneath is ice.'

'Don't blame me for your shortcomings,' she was stung to retaliate.

'What's that supposed to mean?'

'During our courtship, you convinced me I was cold. It took a man of sensitivity to show me that I'm not.'

'You are cold. You're incapable of melting.'

'If that's what you want to think.'

'I can't believe it! You led me on all that time. You can't have known him two seconds, because you certainly weren't two-timing me, and I do believe you've slept with him.'

Ros was regretting drawing out Jarvis. She had attacked his masculinity, and he wasn't going to let her get away with that. He intended to avenge himself. She wasn't going to be able to escape without causing an ugly scene. Abhorrent as the idea of that was, she knew she had no other choice.

She couldn't believe her good fortune when a hand tapped Jarvis on the shoulder and a male voice said, 'I'm cutting in.' By the time he added, 'Is that all right with you, Miss Seymour?' Ros was already in Edward Banks's arms, beaming a smile of gratitude that radiated halfway across the room.

'Ros,' she said, 'please call me Ros. I'll just

call you Sir Galahad.'

He laughed. 'You looked as if you needed rescuing. He seemed very steamed up.'

'My fault. I baited him, and what's more I enjoyed doing it.'

'He must have deserved it.'

'He did!'

'That's emphatic.'

'It still doesn't excuse me. I very nearly caused a dreadful scene in someone else's house. Miles would have taken it in stride, but Hannah would have been horrified.'

'Hannah?'

'Miles's sister.' Assuming that he had merely lost sight of their hostess for a moment, Ros said, 'She's over there, looking her usual lovely self. Between the man in the blue velvet jacket and the girl in red. Do you see her?'

'Ah . . . yes!'

'Blondes always look fantastic in black, don't you think?'

'Not all blondes, but that one certainly does.' His eyes were full of lively appreciation. 'Hannah is a very striking woman.'

When the record ended. Miles appeared. 'Edward, my dear fellow, I'm afraid I'm neglecting my duties as a host. I haven't introduced you to anyone yet. If I may drag you away from Ros, I'll take you on the rounds. Hopefully, I won't flounder. In a crush like this, names get evasive, and I get confused over who are our friends and who are friends'

friends. At this time of the year, people seem to have house guests, and I always say, "bring them with you." The more the merrier is my motto.'

Miles's air of discomfort on meeting Edward earlier in the day was considerably less noticeable, yet there was still something that puzzled her. Just before they walked away, Miles's eyes seemed to flash a message at her that she couldn't understand. She must remember to ask him what it was all about.

At a later point in the evening, as she was talking to Hannah, Ros was amused to see Hannah looking at Edward Banks with the same kind of approving interest in her eye that had been in his when he'd looked at her.

'Your friend is a very good-looking man,' Hannah said.

'My friend?'

'Well, he certainly befriended you over that incident with Jarvis. It was looking nasty until he intervened.'

'You saw that? Jarvis isn't a good loser. He wanted us to get back together. I should have said no, very firmly, and kept on saying no, and nothing else, until he was convinced. I unwisely let him know there is someone else.'

'I knew it! I could tell that something about you was different when you walked in yesterday. So why don't I feel pleased for you?'

'Because you sense things. You always know that bit more than you're told, or so it seems.

162

There's no future for us.'

'You mean there's some obstacle that prevents you from marrying?'

'He doesn't believe in marriage. That's an obstacle, I suppose. But that isn't it. I don't know whether you know any of this or not, but my father tried to phone me. When he couldn't get hold of me, he phoned Miles and asked him to pass on a message. A man he was working with contracted some obscure illness for which there's no cure. He said there was a chance that he might look me up. I presume my father prompted this thinking that the man could use some company, the idea being for me to cheer him up.'

'Only you went a step further than that?'

'Yes. I fell in love with him. Would you blame me for . . . well . . . snatching what happiness with him I can?'

'I think you are going to be hurt. But no, I wouldn't blame you. I would like to think I'd be the same myself. Miles told me about your father's phone call, of course. We were both terribly sickened. Look, Rosalynd, I must go and do my hostess bit. We'll talk about this later, m'm?'

People were now beginning to drift away. Once again, Edward Banks sought Ros out.

'Before I go, I just want you to know how much I've enjoyed this evening and what a pleasure it's been to meet you.'

Meet you, he said. Not see you again.

'So we hadn't met before today?'

'No. Did you think we had?'

'Yes. You didn't approach me like a stranger.'

'That's because you don't seem like a stranger to me. I've heard so much about you from you-know-who that I felt we were old acquaintances. All that's been said about you is true. You *are* a lady of beauty, charm and talent.'

'Miles goes on too much. I don't aspire to beauty, and neither am I all that talented. I'm only a glorified home economist.'

'Yes, Miles is very proud of you, too,' he said, making her wonder who else had been singing her praises. 'Your modesty becomes you. But you're rather more than that. Author of a very successful string of cookbooks, television personality.'

She declaimed, 'Hardly that. I was asked to tape a show before a selected studio audience. They liked me. So I was invited back to complete the series. I've just one more program to record. The audience ratings when it's screened will say whether I'm asked back again or not. I'm not sure that I want it, anyway. I prize my obscurity.'

'I'm confident that the choice will be yours. If I'm around, I'll be sure to watch out for you.'

'Oh, are you going away?'

He pursed his mouth. 'Two days ago, I

would have given a decisive yes. Now there's a slender chance that I might be staying my allotted time, after all.'

*　　*　　*

The last guest had departed. Hannah yawned delicately behind her hand, gracious to the end. 'Leave the clearing up, Rosalynd. I'll do it tomorrow.'

She meant that her cleaning lady would do it the next day. Imagining the poor woman coming in to all this mess, Ros said, 'I want to do it. You've done enough. Put your feet up, and watch someone else work.'

'Don't I always? I'm a past master at the gentle art of delegation, but if you insist,' Hannah said. Ending on a smug note, she added, 'Didn't everything go beautifully?'

'Nothing unusual about that,' Ros said with the utmost sincerity. 'Your parties are always rather special.'

'But of course!' Hannah smiled. 'That's because we're special people, don't you agree, Miles?'

'I invariably do agree with you, Hannah, dear. In this instance, the chief accolade must go to Edward Banks. The courage of that guy. Makes you feel sort of humble. I know if that sentence hung over me, I wouldn't be as genial. A bear with a sore thumb would have nothing on me.'

165

'Sentence?' Ros queried. 'He's not in trouble with the law, is he?' Miles and Hannah exchanged telling looks. The air was electric.

Miles let out his breath in a rush. 'I thought you were doing so well. I've been praising you to myself all evening and wondering how you managed to be so perfectly natural with him. I even tried to follow your example. And now I see it wasn't a bit of good acting at all. You didn't know!'

Hannah was suddenly sitting up, looking very tense as she scrutinized Ros's face. 'Is that true?'

Her head was spinning. She remembered Miles's using that expression before and completed it in her mind. Under sentence *of death.* 'I must have had too much to drink,' she said. 'I'm not usually this much of a cloth head.'

'I'll vouch for that,' Hannah said, 'but not for the reason you've given. You've hardly touched a drop all evening.'

'Oh—you take note of what your guests drink, do you?'

'You know better than that. Providing they're not driving themselves home, they can drink themselves insensible for all I care. I know you. Half a glass and that's your limit. Stop dodging the issue.'

'Sorry. I'm a coward. I think I've reasoned it out, but . . . it's so wonderful that I can't believe it's true. Not that it's so wonderful for

166

Edward if it is true. Because . . . he is the man my father phoned about'—her eyes shot pleadingly to Miles—'isn't he?'

'Yes. I can't make head, tail or middle of your confusion. It doesn't make sense why you don't know. I told you his name when you phoned from Yorkshire.'

Miles had known from the beginning. That's why he'd been so distressed when he'd first met Edward. He hadn't known what line to take.

'I didn't catch his name. The connection was so bad I only heard half of what you said. When I phoned you back later to find out the bits I'd missed, I'd already met Cliff, and everything fitted. He had just come back from Saudi Arabia, and he was on sick leave. He told me he'd got malaria, but I didn't believe him. I thought that was just a cover-up. I was firmly convinced in my mind that he was the man my father phoned about.'

'But your father isn't in Saudi Arabia. He's in Australia,' Miles corrected.

'I know that now. Australia. Saudi Arabia. It's easy to mistake one for the other on a bad line, and that's what I did. With disastrous consequences. Poor Edward.' Her brow went thoughtful. 'I've just remembered something rather odd that Edward said. On thinking about it, it could be hopeful. We were talking about the series I'm doing for television. He said he'd watch out for it if he were still around. I asked him if he was going away, and he said that two days ago he would have said yes but now there was a slender chance that he might not be going. Do you know what he meant by that, Miles?'

'Yes. He confided in me. Having come to terms with the other, he's trying not to build his hopes up too high in case it doesn't come off, but apparently there's some new treatment they want to try him on. A new wonder drug that's only recently come on the market.'

'I hope it works. I'll pray for it. It's got to work.'

'He'll have to go into the hospital for a while; they want him under constant observation. I said I'd visit him. Now you can fill me in on something that's got me guessing.'

'What's that?'

'Who is Cliff?'

'Now you're the one who's not being very bright,' Hannah chipped in on a chiding note. 'It's as obvious as the nose on your face who he is.'

'It isn't to me.'

'Cliff is the reason for the stars shining bright enough to blind you in this little girl's eyes. He is the man she has fallen in love with.'

'I didn't know Ros had fallen in love with anyone. I thought she was still falling out of love with Jarvis. No one tells me anything,' he grumbled.

'Why should they? You only have control of

her business interests. Rosalynd's private life is her own affair. Go to bed, Miles.'

He got to his feet. He'd spotted the gleam in his sister's eye and knew from past experience there was little use in resisting her domination, although at the door he did turn and say: 'Take your own advice, Hannah, and don't pry.'

'Shoo. I never pry. I show kindly concern. There's a difference.'

The door closed behind him. Hannah turned to Ros.

'Where do you go from here?'

'Back to Yorkshire for my things. Apart from the bits and bobs I've brought with me to cover this trip, everything I possess is up there. Then I'll do a smart U-turn and come back here. Not to stay as a permanency, I need a place of my own. But I'd be grateful if you'd put me up for a day or two, until I find somewhere. Will you?'

'You don't have to ask. You're always welcome here, but why?'

'Could it be because I'm not a lot of trouble and try to be the perfect guest?'

'Not that why, you idiot. Presuming that Cliff is staying in Yorkshire. Is he?'

'Yes, to the best of my knowledge,' Ros qualified. 'I've gone off jumping to conclusions.'

'I don't blame you for that. But I do blame you for the other. Why, now that everything is

169

right and he isn't going to die, are you going to put all that distance between you?'

'You're a very astute woman, Hannah. I think you've a good idea why.' She wasn't going to confuse the issue even further with a lengthy explanation about the mix-up of the cottages, which meant they were living under the same roof, and so she admitted simply, 'We haven't made love yet, not all the way, but it nearly happened. I wanted it to happen, and I resolved that when I returned, I'd see that it did happen.'

'Should I be shocked, Rosalynd? Is that what you expect me to be? I'm not.'

But Ros was shocked. It sounded so bold, so brazen. 'That was before, when I thought he was going to die. I couldn't now . . . and if I went back to stay, it would be difficult not to . . . because . . .' She thought that perhaps she would do a bit more explaining. So, after all, she went right back to the beginning and told Hannah about the repairs being carried out on the wrong cottage and how she had gone to seek a bed for the night with a friendly neighbor, only to find Cliff in residence and not his grandmother. 'My own cottage isn't habitable yet, and the repairs can't get under way until the weather picks up, whenever that will be. I can't go back and live under the same roof as him, not now everything's changed. Before, it was no good my wanting marriage, I couldn't expect it of a man who didn't have a

170

future to offer me. But Cliff has a future. He could marry me if he wanted to. There's no obstruction apart from his refusal to enter into a commitment. I feel so angry with him, and I'm going to feel a lot angrier when I get over my relief that he's not going to die.'

'You said you wanted it to happen between you. Do you still want it? Truthfully now.'

'Yes.'

'Correct me if I'm wrong, but as I see it, you want the same thing that you are condemning him for wanting.'

'It's not like that.'

'Isn't it? What is it like, then?'

Ros knew what was behind the interrogation, what Hannah was hinting at. She felt her cheeks going pink, and she couldn't think what to say; no plausible explanation would come to mind to justify why her lust was any different from Cliff's lust. 'It's . . . different. Because I want to legalize it, that's why,' she finished triumphantly.

'Everything's got to be tidy, hasn't it, Rosalynd? It's all right if it's tidy. It was all right when you thought Cliff was going to die. You could fool yourself that you were giving yourself to him as an act of supreme and unimpeachable self-sacrifice. The doing of it was above reproach because the motive behind it was of such a highly commendable nature. Now that you can't redeem your desire on that score, you're looking for another tidy way out.

171

Marriage.'

'That's unfair. Haven't you been listening? I've wanted marriage from the beginning. I thought he couldn't plan for the future because he didn't have a future to plan for. That's what's making me so furious.'

'I don't see why it should. You've admitted to me that he's been straight with you. He hasn't tried to take you in.'

'No.' Ros frowned. 'I've taken myself in, and that's worse. I set out to seduce him! He told me I'd be getting a rotten bargain. My virginity for his lust. He told me he couldn't give me a commitment. I thought he was being very noble and selfless in turning me down. And stop smiling, Hannah, it isn't funny.'

'No, dear. Sorry. Did he really turn you down?'

'He was pretty feeble about it. He soon made it clear that he was willing to be worked on to change his mind. I've been so gullible. The toad even told me he was a toad. Well . . . frog actually . . . practically the same.'

'A what did you say?'

'A frog. It was one of those joke things between us. He said he wasn't likely to turn into my prince and that he was a frog through and through. Afterward, we pulled a box of crackers. In one of them there was a joke slip about it being a girl's lot to kiss a lot of frogs in her search for her prince. We fell about laughing.'

'He sounds to be a lot of fun.'

'Sure. And the laugh's on me.'

'Your Cliff puts me in mind of a man I used to know,' Hannah continued unperturbed. 'He was a lot of fun, too. I had the same kind of sparkle about me that you have now. I lit up for him, just as you light up for Cliff. I was very young, younger than you are, only just eighteen. He was considerably older, which added a certain spice to our friendship. Before him, I'd only known boys of my own age. How callow they seemed once I was in the company of an experienced man of the world. He made me feel so alive. One hour of his company was worth twenty of anyone else's.'

'What happened?' Ros asked, perking up and taking notice. She'd always known there was someone special in Hannah's life who had spoiled her for other men.

'What happened?' Hannah repeated. 'Nothing. I wouldn't let it happen, because I was very foolish. You call yourself gullible. So was I. I was so gullible I believed everything anybody told me. He told me that he was a confirmed bachelor, that he would never settle down with a wife and raise a brood of children. He said he wasn't cut out to be a family man. And I believed him. As I wanted all the things that were so abhorrent to him, I ended our friendship. Friendship, Rosalynd, I never permitted it to be a relationship, although if I'm honest with myself I would have liked to

173

have had a relationship with him, in the fullest sense of the word. Like you, I was a coward. I needed a sop for my conscience, something to make it tidy and acceptable. Of course, I'm going back to a time when attitudes weren't as free and easy as they are now. I was afraid of shocking people. I loved him, but I loved my good name more. So we parted.'

'Is there something else? I've a feeling there is.'

'Oh, yes, quite an amusing little epilogue. I met him again, many years later. He was with his wife and his four delightful children. Never have I seen a more besotted husband or as proud a father.'

'It's a touching story. But it won't make any difference to me.'

'I didn't expect it to. There are many injustices in this life, but in one respect it's fair. We all have to learn by our own mistakes.'

## CHAPTER NINE

It began to snow again as Ros headed back for Yorkshire. She switched on the car radio and listened to the dismal announcement of freezing fog, snow and black ice. The farther north she traveled, the worse the conditions. She wanted to put her foot down and get there as quickly as possible, but common sense told her that would be a short cut to the nearest hospital, and so she went easy on the accelerator pedal.

She was still dazed by the turn of events, her sadness for Edward Banks mingling with her joy that it wasn't Cliff. She prayed earnestly that it would come out all right for Edward, that the treatment would work and he would be given a new lease on life. And how precious that life would be. He would view each day as a miracle and never again take his existence for granted. She didn't know that he ever had, only that it was common knowledge that most people do.

Her happiness that it wasn't Cliff knew no bounds. Even as she raged inwardly at herself for jumping to the conclusion that she had—and everything had interlocked so convincingly that she had been positive that Cliff was the man her father had phoned about—she didn't regret everything. She knew that by asking herself just one question. Say she was vested with some strange power that allowed her to give this Christmas back, never to have known the wonder and fun of that idyllic time with Cliff, would she use it? The answer was no! That time was fiercely precious to her. So then she asked herself another question. If she refused to deny herself what had been, why was she denying herself what could be even better now that the sadness was erased? She'd discovered firsthand that women have the

175

same feelings, desires, as men. Only a man puts the demands of his body first, whereas a woman must appease her conscience before she can satisfy the urges of her body. She was up against the fundamental difference of the sexes.

Her indignation took a sharp climb. Why should she be the one to give in? Wasn't her pride every bit as important as Cliff's unreasonable reluctance to commit himself? It wasn't just a matter of pride, but a question of caring. Not just hers, but Cliff's as well. Some of the caring had to be on his side. If he wouldn't, or couldn't, give her his love, she couldn't settle for his lust.

It was dark by the time she arrived at the cottage. Cliff must have been listening for her, as he had on that other occasion when she came back from phoning Miles, her heart in anguish because of what she'd heard. It was like a replay of an old film, she thought, as the cutting of the car engine triggered off the opening of the cottage door and Cliff came striding forward to greet her. Cold and despondent, with her heart no longer in anguish but frozen in anger, she got out of the driving seat, slammed the car door shut as though taking some of her vengeance out on it and trudged forward to meet him.

'You look chilled to the core,' he said, tucking her under the protection of his arm.

She didn't seem able to summon up the

energy to thrust it off. 'I had to drive with the car window down for most of the way to be able to see.'

He shuttled her through the door. Just as she hadn't been able to push off his arm, so she couldn't push off the sensation of coming home. It wedged in her throat and made swallowing difficult. And that was nothing to the mammoth difficulty that faced her. She would have to get the message across to Cliff, the sooner the better, before his forceful character melted her resistance.

He sat her down on the same kitchen chair as before and removed her boots. He had put her slippers out in readiness, and he took each foot in turn and slid it into the blissful warmth.

He dealt with her gloves and unbuttoned her coat, saying, 'We'll soon have the blood circulating.'

'I'm not staying, Cliff.'

His eyebrows contested that remark.

'Tonight, yes,' she amended, submitting to having her coat removed. 'I'm not foolish enough to drive straight back again. I've come for my things, and I'm leaving in the morning.'

'What are you talking about?'

'No mystery, just what I said. I head south again tomorrow.'

'I won't let you go.'

She waved a ringless hand in front of his face. 'It works both ways, Cliff. You can't have a commitment on one side and none on the other. We are both free agents. You can't stop me from going.'

'I see. It's that, is it?' His mouth twisted in cynicism. 'What am I supposed to do now? Go down on my bended knees and ask you to marry me? Is that what you expect?'

'I don't expect anything from you, Cliff. That way I won't be disappointed.'

She sighed in near desperation. 'I'm sorry, Cliff, but I'm not interested in a casual affair.'

'There is nothing casual about our feelings for one another, and you insult us both by suggesting there is.'

'It was Christmas. We were flung together in the season of good will. What else could you expect? But Christmas is over, Cliff.'

'Don't you believe it! Nothing's over. It's just beginning. There might have been an element of chance in the way we met up again, but proximity didn't take us into one another's arms, the force of our own emotions drove us there.'

She hadn't missed his reaction about the Christmas dig. She'd stumbled on that line by accident and didn't see why she shouldn't make the most of it, even as her sense of self-preservation appealed for caution.

'It was better than playing noughts and crosses,' she said, shrugging her shoulders to imply indifference, surrendering to the unwise delight of goading him.

'Why you—' His jaw tightened, his hands

reached out and pulled her to her feet, and then she was held meltingly close in his arms.

Their views clashed violently, his opinion of the worthless state of marriage was repugnant to her, but she couldn't find his nearness repellent. Physically, they were on the same wave length.

He had proved his point by setting her pulses racing and firing her blood with wild expectancy; but the kiss her mouth yearned for did not materialize as his hold loosened and his head drew away to look at her. 'Did that feel casual, Ros? Didn't you want more?'

Declining to answer that, stepping back to put some needful distance between them, she said, 'You give it a casual flavor by avoiding a decision.'

'You can't charge me with that and make it stick. I could have drifted along and kept you guessing. I made a decision, long before I met you, not to sink up to my ears into domesticity. I never conned you on that score.'

'I conned myself,' she said bitterly. 'It was all my fault. I can lay no blame at your door.'

'My kind of work will always take me away from home for a spell. I've seen too many of my mates taken in by cheating wives. It's not going to happen to me. I'll tell you the pattern. At first, the new bride goes with her husband, but then the children begin to arrive. Wife stays home, gets lonely, seeks adult male company.'

179

'One rotten apple doesn't mean the whole barrel's tainted. All women aren't alike. And while we're about it, how many of your mates cheat on their wives?'

'Fair comment. You're better off not getting tied up with the likes of me. If I was the marrying kind, there's no one with whom I'd rather plight my troth, believe me.'

'Sorry, but I don't find that much of a compliment. As for the bit about plighting your troth—'she laughed—'what an archaic description.'

'I used it deliberately. It fits an archaic institution. In my opinion, trust is more important.'

'Trust in what? That you don't get tired of me and send me packing in under six months? A year, or whatever? I find this argument rather pointless. You keep your views, and I'll stick to mine.'

A puzzled frown creased his forehead. 'You knew my views before. You might not have accepted them, but they didn't stand between us. You never froze me off because of them.'

'Ah . . . well. There was a reason.'

'Which, if I'm any judge of that mutinous look on your face, you're not telling.'

'Too true, I'm not.'

'Something's happened during the time you were away.'

'Top marks again for a correct observation.'

'You've seen your old boy friend again.'

She had never told him of the complete reversal of her feelings for Jarvis. When he'd first made the suggestion that they share Holly Cottage, she'd kept her thoughts on that score to herself, feeling that if the situation got out of hand, it would serve as some kind of protection to let him think that she was still pining for her ex-fiancé. His male arrogance would never permit him to make love to a woman whose affections were held by another man.

So she smiled, letting her lashes slide down as though protective of a look of dreamy reminiscence in her eyes as her thoughts lingered on her recent meeting with Jarvis. 'Brilliant,' she said on a breathy laugh. 'Miles and his sister, Hannah, always throw a New Year's Day party. Jarvis was there.'

'And you got chummy again?'

A small, gloating smile possessed her mouth. 'We talked.'

'And he wants to patch things up between you?'

'He wants to marry me,' she said.

'Liar.'

'I beg your pardon!'

'Oh, I don't mean about his wanting to marry you. I'll take your word on that. I mean this touching little performance you're giving is a lie. He might have ignited a small glimmer of feeling in you once, I won't dispute that fact, either. But the fire we lit together blew it out.'

181

The way he tore down her arguments, slashed through her defenses, horrified her. Drawing back her shoulders, lifting her chin at him in defiance, she began, 'Your conceit is—'

'—completely justified.' His searching glance compelled her eyes to meet his and submit to the cruelly penetrating look he gave her. 'You're not a shallow person, Ros. Feelings run deep in you. You might have thought you were once in love with Jarvis when you didn't know any better, before your senses were excited and you were in complete physical harmony with a man for the first time. The tongue can lie, the heart can play you false, but the senses can always be relied upon to spell out the truth. Feelings can't be faked. And neither do you have to search for them like words, or truth even. It's something you know, an instinctive reaction that hits you.' His fingers reached forward and scraped down her cheek. The electric tingle encompassed every part of her body. 'What do you feel, Ros?'

'Nothing,' she said, her voice little more than a croak.

'Then I shall have to carry the demonstration a step further.'

'Don't touch me!' The words that should have been screamed at him came out sounding more like a plea.

'Why mustn't I touch you?'

'Because it doesn't please me any more.'

'Oh? What does it do to you?'

182

'It fills me with revulsion.' The revulsion was against herself for being so weak where he was concerned, for not having the strength of character to be cold and indifferent toward him.

'No, Ros, that isn't true. When you feel revulsion toward a person, it's just about impossible not to show it. If you stand too close to them, your inclination is to cringe away. You don't cringe away from me, not deep down inside. It's all a pretense, Ros, an ill-concealed covering for what you really want, which is for me to take you into my arms. Your lips are hungry for mine, your body yearns to experience fully the sweet delights it has been awakened to.'

'Why, you monster!'

'Is that an improvement on a frog, I wonder. Perhaps frogs are your preference, Ros. To hear you talk, Jarvis has suddenly turned into your prince, but I bet you can't even stand him near you. It might even have crossed your mind to wonder how you ever could. Not that he ever got that close to you. An engaged couple sharing a platonic relationship!' His dry laugh was insulting. 'That tells its own story.'

'It wasn't that platonic,' she said, retaliating to that smug, taunting look.

He couldn't know for sure. Or could he? He didn't just look at her but into her mind. It was as if he could read beyond her own thoughts and see into compartments of her brain that baffled her. He couldn't know her better than she knew herself! And in this instance, it was just blind guesswork.

'You're bluffing, Cliff. You want to believe so hard that it didn't happen between me and Jarvis that you'd fall over backward to convince yourself. But you don't know. And there's no way you ever can know for sure.'

'Isn't there?'

Before she could possibly realize what he had in mind to do, she was swept into his arms, and his mouth came down on hers, stemming any protest she might have made and highlighting the truth of all he had said. Feelings are beyond the power of human control. Hers swamped her as the driving passion of his kiss carried her into a vortex of pure pleasure. Much to her own *dis*pleasure. She had revealed herself to him before her brain had had a chance to signal to her emotions that it was against her wishes. She willed her body to stiffen in rejection as it had when she danced in Jarvis's arms. She clamped her mouth so tightly shut to him that her jaw and cheek bone ached with the tension it inflicted upon them. This belated reaction brought a smile to the mouth that had briefly drawn away from hers, and with it came a change of tactics. The steel grip of his arms became a more gentle trap as his hands played along the rigidity of her spine, his fingertips burning through the thickness of her sweater.

184

His mouth covered hers with light butterfly kisses that tantalized and excited and left her feeling dissatisfied.

Not only did it melt her sham resistance, it was all she could do not to cling to him and let her traitorous mouth beg for the passion it had previously known. But that would offer only partial appeasement, and it wouldn't be long before her body was crying out for parity. It remembered the joy of being molded to his desire by hands that coaxed and demanded by turn, a subtle variance that goaded her into active response as it made her long to yield to his male dominance. He was clever and devious and persuasive, and her inflexible will was putty in his hands.

'See what I mean,' he said, and she could cheerfully have hit him. 'You are a straightforward idealist, Ros. Nothing happened between you and Jarvis that a third party couldn't have observed. It isn't in your makeup to amuse yourself with a man you don't feel deeply about, and you couldn't feel for Jarvis and be warm and responsive in my arms. I've made some supper. A hot-pot, because I thought you'd need something to thaw you out after your long journey. Let's eat, and then we'll go to bed.' He didn't say *together*, but the implication was there.

He knew all the answers. She had only one answer, and he had no intention of asking the question that fitted it. She hated him for what he did to her. She was also very hungry. Perhaps inner sustenance would give her the strength to resist him. At all costs, she must stay out of his bed and keep him out of hers.

'You had your chance. You passed it up.'

'Yes.' He frowned. 'To my dying day, I'll wonder why.'

To work, the kind of no-strings relationship he had in mind had to be acceptable to both parties. He had spoken one truth too many, to his own detriment. Her feelings did run deep. When she went swimming, she never paddled in the shallow end, she swam where the water was over her head, and this corresponded with her emotions. She was already in deeper than she cared for. It would be a long time, if ever, before she got over Cliff. The longer she let it linger on, the harder it would be when the parting eventually came.

It was a very good hot-pot. As they ate her thoughts ran on. Despite what he'd said, she had gotten to him about Jarvis. He had no idea how accurately he had hit the nail on the head about her waning interest in her ex-fiancé, and so against all the odds, he was jealous. Was there anyone in his life whom she ought to be jealous of?

'Cliff?'

'Yes?'

'Have you never been in love?'

'Not to my knowledge.'

Breaking off a chunk of bread ready to pop

into her mouth, she said, 'You haven't, then. If you'd been in love, you'd know for definite.'

A cross appeared between his heavy black brows, drawing them more closely together. 'You still don't think that milk-and-water affection you had for Jarvis was love, do you?'

It might have been in her best interest to keep that pot boiling, but she was a stickler for the truth, and so she was forced to admit, 'No.'

'I'm assuming there was no one before Jarvis?'

'No.'

'So how can you know whether or not I'd know if I'd ever been in love, never having been in that state yourself? The only way you would be in a position to know would be if you'd been in love.'

Had it never crossed his mind to wonder if she was in love with him, or was that what he was angling to find out? That was one secret better kept to herself.

'Because I'm a woman,' she replied, 'and women know about these things. I don't suppose you believe in feminine intuition any more than you believe in marriage.'

'No, I don't. Neither can I understand your constant preoccupation with marriage.'

'Know something? When I look at you, neither can I. I think it's as well you hold the views you do. You've saved some poor girl a very unhappy life. And now I'm going to wash the supper things and take my weary self to bed.'

'Want company?'

'I thought I'd already made it outstandingly clear that I'm sleeping on my own.'

'You've got a one-track mind. I meant with the washing up.'

'You didn't, you know.'

'Perhaps not,' he said darkly, watching her stack the cutlery on to the plates, and then he picked up the tureen the hot-pot had been in and followed her into the kitchen.

'Something's got me really puzzled, Ros.'

'What's that?' she asked in slight trepidation, not caring for the sharply discerning look that had come to his face. It made her nervous.

'I've been recalling how you were as a child. You were so honest, on occasion it hurt—and frequently you were the one it hurt. You wouldn't shirk the truth, even to avoid a scolding or worse. There was no deception about you, no wheedling little tricks or resorting to guile to get your own way. And in this respect you haven't altered one bit. You're still truthful and straight dealing to the point of self-destruction. Oh, you might fall back upon the odd permitted evasion that marks your sex, because women are notoriously equivocal creatures, but you are totally without subterfuge in the issues that are important.'

'Where is this leading, Cliff?' she asked, her nervousness increasing. She tried not to draw her tongue over her lips or make any gesture that might give some hint of her feelings.

'I admit that at first I did wonder if you were giving me a sample taste of the goods to sell the whole product. But I soon realized that wasn't so. I know you too well. It's not your style to resort to tactics. You didn't set out to make yourself indispensable to me to force my hand. You didn't come into my bed and offer yourself to me to trap me into marriage, did you? Did you?' he insisted when she made no reply.

'You're the one with the answers, so why ask me?' she said, falling back on prevarication, which he seemed to interpret as provocation.

'Because I want to hear it from you.' His eyes concentrated wickedly on her mouth, as if he knew that it had suddenly gone as dry as though she were trying to swallow razor blades. The compulsion to lick her lips was almost unbearable. But then he lost ground by revealing the temper smoldering under his seemingly benign manner, showing that he was not so unruffled and in control, after all. 'Confound it, you'll tell me even if I have to beat it out of you.'

'How do you know what my style is?' she said, shooting home the advantage he had unexpectedly given her. 'I would have said that using violence against a woman wasn't your style.'

'You're not acting like a woman,' he ground out savagely. 'I understand women. You're behaving like a pixilated child, and that's what's thrown me. Now answer me, so help me or—' He grabbed hold of her wrists, holding them so tightly she wondered they didn't snap, and yanked her forward, his eyes, above hers, dark shafts of menace. 'You didn't come into my bed to force a marriage proposal out of me, did you?'

'No!' she shrieked at him, fearing to ignite his anger further but shrinking in apprehension of the question she knew would inexorably follow.

'So why did you come into my bed and offer your delicious self to me as a gift?' he said, turning the joking way she had put it when she went to him into an insult.

Even so, her desire to lash back at him was tempered with kindness. She couldn't tell him the reason why. And so, lifting a defiant chin at him, she countered, 'Could it be because I felt it was time I got myself some—'she was going to say experience but chopped it off and said instead—'form of comparison.'

'That was one of the permitted feminine evasions I just spoke of. Not very good, was it?' he sneered. 'You need to practice harder to get it right, but on some other guy. Don't try it on with me.'

'And don't you threaten me. Oh, I'm perfectly well aware that you could bully the truth out of me, but let me tell you this, if you do you won't like it.'

'Try me.'

'All right. It's good enough for you. I don't know why I tried to spare your feelings. I came to you out of compassion. Or if you like—pity!'

'Pity! I thought I'd heard everything. But that's a new one on me. What kind of stupid answer is that?'

'I wanted to give you some comfort.'

'Now you're really getting under my skin. Cut the smart talk.'

'It's the truth. You're hurting me. What are you trying to do—brand me? If you'll stop using brute force on me,' she said, impotently trying to shake his hands off her wrists, 'and sit down and listen to me in a reasonable manner, I'll explain how the misunderstanding came about.'

'Very well,' he said, his hands dropping from her, the surprise on his face showing that he had barely been aware that he had subjected her to such a cruel hold.

Tomorrow she would have finger bruises on her wrists, now she rubbed each one in turn to get the circulation going, which brought a fresh wave of displeasure to his face. Apparently, it was in order for him to ill use her but not acceptable for her to draw attention to it.

'I thought you were going to die,' she said, rubbing her wrists harder in bravado.

'I am. So are you. Everyone dies eventually.'

'Don't mock. Listen!' she called out hotly. 'I thought your death was coming quite soon.'

She went on to explain fully, and this time he listened without interrupting her. She had been wrong about a lot of things, but she had been right in thinking he would not be pleased at her reason for going to him. She might have been selflessly drawn to do what she did in the first place, but Hannah had got it right and her compassion for him had quickly turned into unimaginable delight for her, but she wasn't going to tell him that. She enjoyed watching him squirm, seeing the dark color flood into his cheeks as fury held his features rigid.

When she'd finished, he didn't speak for a moment. Then his savage eyes slid down her body, stripping her insolently before coming back to rest in taunting derision on her face. 'This Edward Banks. Presumably you offered him the same comfort. Minus gift wrapping. A gift that had been prehandled, but I don't suppose he would demur too much about that.'

Taking a clamp on her rising temper, her mouth shaped to sweetness. 'What's that to you? In any case, isn't that a rather cowardly way of hitting back? I didn't want to tell you. You insisted on knowing the truth. I'm sorry it wasn't to your liking.'

'Like hell you are.' His voice had now gone ominously quiet.

His eyes narrowed in concentrated thought.

He hadn't finished with her yet. It would be safer for her to do the washing up in record time and get out of the kitchen before he decided on what line to take. It went against her fastidious streak to leave the dishes until morning, although when she saw him reach for the drying cloth, she realized that's what she ought to have done. Unlike her, he never ran true to form. She had expected him to say, '*Damn* you to hell,' or even some more robust expletive and storm out of the kitchen, slamming the door behind him with enough force to shake it off its hinges. This quiet, controlled violence as he worked by her side was unnerving.

'You don't have to help,' she said. 'I can manage the dishes on my own.'

'I'm sure you can. I like to do my share.'

'You prepared the meal. That was doing more than your share.'

'If you say so,' he said, putting the cloth down but not moving away.

She bent her head, feigning absorption in her task, sinking her hands deep into the sudsy water. She heard the shuffle of his footsteps and took a deep breath, thinking he was going, and held it as it was brought forcibly home to her that he had merely shifted position to stand behind her. His hands came round her waist, drawing her back against him.

'Go away, Cliff.'

His mouth nuzzled under her hair and made

teasing bites along her neck. 'Send me away. You can now that you know I'm not going to die, not before my allotted time, anyway.'

'If someone doesn't kill you first.'

'All you have to say is, "Go away, Cliff."'

'Are you deaf? I've just said it.'

'But you've got to mean it. Say, "Go away, Cliff," and mean it. Surely that's not very difficult? You don't have to endure my odious attentions now that you no longer feel pity for me. Or perhaps,' he said, his fingers sliding under her sweater and layering themselves against her rib cage, 'you don't find this odious?'

'I never said I did.'

'No, you didn't. Perhaps you find it exciting. The story you've just spun out is too incredible not to be true. In any case, it's already been agreed between us that you wouldn't lie about anything of that magnitude.'

'I did come to you out of compassion,' she said doggedly.

'And for how long was compassion uppermost in your mind? I didn't hold a passive female in my arms. You found me as physically desirable as I found you.'

It hadn't taken him long to reason that out, she thought bitterly, biting heavily on her lower lip to stop herself letting out a yelp of pleasure as his trespassing fingers, having made a slight detour to unfasten her bra, scaled upward to cup both her breasts. The

194

resultant electric thrill that radiated through her was like an adhesive that pressed and held her enraptured body closer to his. It was as if she were trying to melt into the solid torso and the strong muscular legs that were slightly straddled to form an inverted, protective vee round hers and stopped them both from falling over. It took a lot of will power to pull herself away from him and transfer her weight to the edge of the kitchen sink.

'It's your privilege to move away.' His whispery laugh assaulted her ear, the breath from it scalded her neck. 'I don't force myself on any woman. No woman takes me out of pity. You're safe. I'll amend that, as safe as you want to be. How safe do you want to be, Ros?'

A good question.

He turned her round to face him. His hands stroked down over her disarranged sweater in a feeble pretense of straightening it, which made her yearn to be crushed close to his chest. They both knew that she was having to fight off not only him but also her own inflamed senses. His aim would be to keep them inflamed. It had slashed him when she had told him that she'd gone to him out of compassion. It had insulted his masculinity. She would never forget the way his face had changed color, the suppressed fury of him. She had known he would seek vengeance. And this was it, of course. Her punishment for daring to suggest that she had been motivated by pity. He wasn't going to have that. He would work on her without respite until she owned to her own feelings. He knew what those feelings were. Every quivering nerve in her awakened body was a brazen announcement of her craving for him. But that wasn't enough for him. He had made her admit to her reason for going to him, and he wouldn't let up until she admitted to this. He wanted to hear that she wanted him from her own lips. Well, she'd be damned if she would. She wouldn't give him that satisfaction.

She was in no danger for the moment, she knew that. He wouldn't enter her bedroom without invitation, and tomorrow she would be gone. She could surely hold out for the short length of time she would be here.

She lifted her hands and placed them flat against his chest, pushing him away. She hadn't been given time to dry her hands, and the soapy bubbles on them from the washing-up water adhered to his front like the falling snow outside. As she stalked out of the kitchen, her horrified vision was caught and held by the ominous beauty. Big ragged flakes fell to cluster upon the window sill and obliterate the sky.

'I don't think you'll be going anywhere tomorrow,' Cliff said, plucking the thought out of her mind and sending it after her as a parting shot.

# CHAPTER TEN

The radio gave it out about the crisis road conditions that stretched the length and breadth of the country. There wasn't a county that had escaped the arctic blitz. Planes weren't taking off, many roads were impassable, with a fleet of abandoned cars causing further hazards for those who had to travel.

Ros rubbed a circle on the windowpane to look out and hardly needed the announcer's advice to check first if the roads were open before setting off, or better still, stay at home if it were at all possible. The road had disappeared. The boles of trees and the hedgerows had shortened. All she could see was snow, snow and more snow. She didn't have a big enough shovel to dig her car out, even if she were foolhardy enough to risk it. Neither was it just a personal risk. She couldn't take the chance of adding to the burden of the emergency services and motoring organizations, which were already taxed to the limit.

Following her out of the kitchen and into the living room, Cliff said, 'Looks as if we're stuck with one another for a while longer. Fate is a very funny lady. You think you are in charge of your own destiny and find out that you are at the mercy of her capricious whim.'

Cliff had the look of a man who had resigned himself to a situation, only to find that the terms were quite to his liking.

She crossed to the sofa and sat down. 'You're really enjoying this, aren't you?'

He took the chair opposite, lounging back in comfort, as opposed to her taut, ill-at-ease posture. 'It does have its lighter side. I'm sorry that you don't possess a sense of humor to see it.'

'Thank you for your concern, but there's nothing wrong with my sense of humor. It's normal and healthy, unlike yours, which seems to have a perverted twist to it. And will you please stop looking at me.'

'I was brought up to believe that it was polite to look at a person while I was talking to them.'

'There's looking and looking.'

'You don't like the way I look at you? Is that what you're saying?'

'Yes.'

'Then you shouldn't be so nice to look at. Did you know that you look sexier when you're angry?'

The intensity of his preoccupation with her face drew a slash of harsh color across her cheekbones. But when he left off looking at her face, that was worse, because his dark, wicked eyes slid down her body in slow appraisal, lingering overlong on the rise and fall of her breasts. Indignation was making her breathe more rapidly, and she made a desperate bid to modify that, knowing that he was finding it a major source of amusement. It wasn't a kind amusement that mocks in a gentle way, its main concern to tempt a person out of ill-humor. It was cold, laying icy fingers of persecution on her stomach.

Uncrossing the legs that were now the subject of his scrutiny, she jumped up off the sofa. 'I'll make some coffee. Could you drink a cup?'

'If you promise not to put arsenic in it,' he replied.

'Don't put ideas into my head.'

The slow smile twisting up his mouth told her that he knew she had sought for an excuse to get away from him for a while to get control over herself.

There were two escape routes she could take, both of which would take her too close for comfort to where he sat. She chose the one with the wider swing round his chair to get to her target, the door. Keeping her eyes carefully averted from his compelling face, she measured her step and quelled the childish impulse to break into a run. As she drew level with his chair, she risked an under-the-lashes peep out of the corner of her eye. His expression was without expression, indifferent. He wasn't even looking her way, which made it all the more surprising when, without turning his chin, his arm shot out to hook round her waist and pull her over the arm of his chair and down upon his knee. His hand stayed on her waist. His hold was loose, his fingers spread-eagled. Would they clamp like steel bands if she tried to jump up and attempt to free herself? Tried to . . . attempted to? Answering her own question, she thought that's all it would amount to, because she would not be allowed to go. Rather than engage in an undignified scuffle, she thought it was as well to remain passive. As passive as she could be when his touch had triggered off tremors in her stomach that were rising to sabotage and confuse her.

If only she wasn't so aware of him. Even though he petrified her half out of her mind, he was still the most magnetic charmer she had ever met. The dark enchantment of the spell he cast upon her made her senses swim, and her heart beat faster than was good for it. Its excited beat leaped into her throat as his free hand crossed her breast. He did not touch her there, he never intended to. His aim was to make her think that was his target by shaving perilously close, which he did, even calculating correctly just how far she would strain back. Satan himself lurked in his flashing eyes as his hand continued down and pulled the sleeve of her sweater just clear of her wrist, then brought it nearer to his face to inspect the bruises he had inflicted upon her the day before when he gripped her so tightly.

'You were right. I have put my brand on you.'

He didn't have to bruise her flesh to do that. He had put his brand on her the moment they met up again. Even though it was only her body he lusted for, he had reached out and put his name on her heart, and she felt that she would never be free of him again. She might take up with someone else eventually. The desire for masculine company would drive her into another man's arms, but she would never belong to him as she belonged to Cliff.

'I seem to make a habit of ill using you,' he said.

'You don't know your own strength.'

'Or your weakness.' Oh, he knew her weakness all right, the devil. 'I bruise you without knowing about it.' Neither were all the bruises on the flesh, and he knew about that as well. 'First your shoulder and your poor face when I lashed out during that malaria attack I had. Now your wrists.'

'I didn't know you knew about my shoulder. That was concealed from you.'

'I recall an occasion when not one part of you was hidden from my eyes.'

'Don't, Cliff. I can't take it.'

'Can't take what? Remembering how it was? Does it make you want it to be like that between us again?'

She couldn't lie. She couldn't say no,

because she did want it to be like it was—only better.

'It's no good, Cliff.'

'Why are you so stubborn?'

'The same reason that you are.'

Two dominant personalities had clashed. If she stayed for any length of time, Ros knew only too well whose will would break first. She had to get away at the first possible opportunity.

'Life's too short, Ros, to stand on principles.'

'But you're standing on yours, it's only mine you want to trample down.'

'Only because they're about twenty years behind the times. Why won't you own to that?'

'But I do. I hold old-fashioned ideals. There—you've heard it from my own lips. It's a fetish with you, isn't it, making me admit to things? In this instance—so what! I'm basically an old-fashioned girl. I can no more take lovemaking on its own than I could down neat spirits. In both, I need a modifying element.'

'Back to square one—the price tag on your body. Sex in exchange for a commitment.'

She flushed at the base level he brought it down to. 'It might amount to that. But that's not the angle I look at it from. The other way, with no commitment, no strings of any sort, would put too much of a weight on my conscience.'

'I'm going to have to work on that

conscience of yours. It's an old fuddy-duddy. That, or get to work on you and make you forget it.'

His face was turned to her slightly averted cheek, which shivered as his breath touched it. His mouth didn't have far to come to tease the corner of hers, making gentle licking bites that put an intolerable strain on her. He was so clever. That soft persuasion tormented her to want the full passion. How she managed not to give her lips fully to his kiss she would never know. His references to how it had been between them had ignited a flame of excitement within her that she must squash. In wanting it to be like that again, she was her own worst enemy. Her desire was as invidious as a snake and must be struck down before its poison fully penetrated her blood. It would help if she concentrated on the fact that while she thought of it as making love, the term Cliff used was sex—it was nothing more than sexual satisfaction to him. If anything could help her. It was like sinking in quicksand. She wanted to pull out, but she was being sucked down by the turbulence of her own stirred emotions.

She could never be sure what happened next. Did she turn her head, or did Cliff angle his neck to brush her lips more fully with his, for suddenly her whole mouth was being subjected to a battery of light, unsatisfying kisses that drove her crazy for kisses of depth. Pulses began to beat in various parts of her body that she hadn't known existed, roused from a lifetime's dormancy by the wild exhilaration of a sensual hunger she hadn't known possible until Cliff fed it. And which, for all the fine intentions of her upper mind, at base ground level was not taking kindly to the self-inflicted pain of renunciation.

Barely had her lips beat out their message to him before the tormenting, coaxing, goading seduction blazed into a passion of accelerating savagery that was brutal delight, a feast to the hunger of her deprivation. His mouth glanced across her cheek in a moment's respite, his breath as hot as the fire burning within her, and then came back with renewed vigor to work the soft flesh of her lips into a frenzy.

His hands gathered her body closer, sliding across her shoulders and down her back, seeking under her sweater for softer areas to plunder, his kisses growing more urgent, a greedy, rampageous assault that made her gasp. The yielding weakness that engulfed her horrified her. She struggled in a panicky endeavor to fend off the reaction in her own body, which was defeated when his mouth clamped on hers again in a long drugging kiss. It was all too much for her, the feelings she had tried to suppress broke free of the bounds she had so futilely set out to impose and became the dominant power, subservient only to his superior domination. Her fingers rippled

204

through his hair as the fight drained from her, and her mouth became fiercely alive beneath his.

Cradling her on one hip, he removed her sweater and then her bra. She lifted her arms, assisting him in this undressing as a child would, but the breasts his fingers ran fiery rings round were those of a woman peaked to desire, for his desire. They hardened under the burning throb of his lips, betraying to him both the pleasure he gave her and the sweet urges pushing her to surrender to the demanding potency of his body. That he ached to possess her was obvious in the tremor that jerked through him, swift, uncontrollable, filling her with tenderness and surprise, she supposed because she hadn't realized she could move him like that. She had thought endlessly of his strength but had never considered his weakness.

She enclosed his dark head in the circle of her arms, her own flesh trembling in sensual response to the erotic intimacy of his lips, and the restless fever in the hand following the line of her waist, hip and thigh, until she feared her wildly beating heart would run out of control, just as she had.

He pulled her round on top of him, crushing her close. She knew she should resist but couldn't. In the drowning pleasure of the moment, she didn't know how. She was totally defeated, and victory would have been his if he'd taken it without first gloating over his triumph. It shone in his eyes as he drew his head back a fraction to look at her. The overbearing smugness of the smile on his mouth was more than she could stomach as he crowed: 'Isn't this better than cold virtue? How lovely you are. Lovely and warm and mine.'

This infuriating part was, he didn't know he was gloating. He was merely soliciting her agreement that it was better to indulge in physical pleasure than deny oneself on the grounds of conscience.

A quick, bitter rage filled her heart that made it easy for her to free herself of his arms and scramble off his knee, pulling her sweater back on to hide her body from his eyes. He was so surprised, and that was comic and maddening in itself, that he let her go without putting up even a token fight to detain her. He didn't understand why she suddenly sprang away from him.

'I am not lovely or warm, and I am certainly not *yours*,' she denied.

'You were a moment ago—or almost mine.'

She wanted to lash out at him for being right. She wanted to hit back at him for those moments she had lain in his arms responsive to his lovemaking, for bringing her down to eager, trembling submission. For the passion he had aroused in her. For wanting the body she was doing her best to withhold from him for physical appeasement and for shunning the heart she so desperately wanted to give him. She hated him for being almost his, for the easy conquest he had achieved over her, and for his egotism in knowing that it was in his power to do so. So great was the power he held over her that even in her pain and humiliation she still wanted him. Despite everything, it wouldn't take much for her to fly back into his arms. And that would be the ultimate degradation.

'I don't understand you, I don't understand you at all,' he ground out savagely. 'Why did you kiss me like that if you'd no intention of following it through?'

'Following it through? I didn't realize I was committing myself to anything.' The word 'committing' was the one most suited. It might not have been chosen deliberately, but it served to strengthen her determination and hitch her pride up several notches higher. 'I'm afraid I'm a novice. I don't know the rules of the game. But if it's any consolation, I'm catching on fast. Somewhere in this world is the man for me. I'll just have to keep turning stones over until I find him. If the joke slip in the Christmas cracker is right and I have to kiss a lot of frogs in the process, it occurred to me that it might be as well for me to keep my hand in.'

'Why you—'

The end of that sentence blistered her ears

as she ran into the kitchen.

She retired to her room early but didn't really expect to get much sleep that night. Her thoughts were too angry and confused. Why had she had to get tangled up with someone like Cliff? She remembered the way his kisses set her senses on fire and how marvelous it had been when he touched her, discovering the deeply passionate woman she was, a side of her nature that had surprised her and that she still didn't know how to cope with. Her thoughts and feelings ran away with her and wouldn't be suppressed. She felt a gnawing, aching regret that she wasn't at that moment lying pampered and cherished in Cliff's arms and hated herself for it.

She was just in the drifting-off stages of sleep when a knock on her door awakened her, followed by Cliff's voice calling out to her, 'Let me in, Ros. I want to talk to you.'

'Go away, Cliff, please. No more tonight.'

She knew what turn the conversation would take, and she'd had enough of the sweet persecution. If he entered her bedroom, she knew what the outcome would be. She had no fight left in her.

He knocked again. 'Come on, Ros. Be reasonable.'

She stuffed her fingers in her ears and hid her head under the bedclothes, and finally he went away.

He tried to work on her again the following

day, but still she wouldn't give way. The atmosphere inside the cottage was as many degrees below as it was on the snow-bound outside. There was no camaraderie between them. They stopped talking, sharing the same table but eating their meals in frigid silence. On day three, he attempted to talk her round again, without success. Despite her numbness, she felt quite proud of herself.

It was still day three, but dusk's shadows were gathering, as he said with weary resignation: 'You win. All right, I'll marry you.'

She looked at him in astonishment. No words would come.

'I want you, Ros. It's driving me out of my mind. It's an obsession. I've got to have you, it's as simple as that. You have my solemn oath that as soon as the roads are safe enough for us to venture out, we'll get the paper work done. I won't cheat on you there, but don't cheat on me now. I can't take being shut up with you, yet shut out. I keep remembering things, how you were in my arms. I want you back there again. You held out, and it paid off. You can congratulate yourself. I never thought I'd give in and agree to marriage to possess a body I desired. But then, no body has ever turned me on as much as yours does. I want to go to bed with you for a month. I want to sate myself with you, rid myself of this grinding agony. Come to me laughing, Ros, you've got your own way.'

She couldn't believe her ears. Did he honestly think that would suit her, that she, or any woman with a shred of pride or the tiniest spark of spirit, would accept such a bitter and insulting proposal? Being proposed to by the man you loved was supposed to be the most romantic moment of a girl's life. Something that special should have been wrapped up in his heart and given in tenderness.

She was realistic enough to know that passions couldn't stay indefinitely perched on some high and dazzling peak of excitement. There would be days when other demands took priority. When the children were in too boisterous a mood and her head was splitting with the noise or when they were sick and her heart was aching at the silence. Sometimes she'd want to go for a walk, watch television or read a book, but instead there would be buttons to sew on, the laundering to do, a house to clean. When she simply wanted to relax, it could be that she would be expected to provide him with amusing and loving companionship or play hostess and be witty and sociable to his friends. In exasperation, sadness, worry and stress or in plain old boredom, it would be something to have the tender knowledge of his love locked in her heart. She wanted this moment for those times. The magic of it would always be there to fall back on when things didn't quite go according to plan.

She didn't think she was being unreasonable or asking too much. Cliff professed to know her. If he thought that kind of proposal would suffice, it proved that he didn't know her at all. And if he couldn't come up with something better than that, then she didn't want to know him!

'No, Cliff!' The refusal broke from her lips, full of condemnation.

'What do you mean—no?'

'I can't say yes to that proposal.'

'What's wrong with it?'

'If you don't know, I can't tell you.'

He looked puzzled, then angry. 'Look—I've managed to hang on to my freedom for a long time. I've said I'll marry you. What more do you want?'

He seemed to think she ought to be falling all over him in gratitude because of the sublime sacrifice he was making. But what of her sacrifice? It would hardly change things at all for him. Not like the shattering changes it would bring to her. He would have everything he had now. His work, his friends, with the comfortable and homely addition of a wife. But her life would alter drastically. She was luckier than most females in the flexibility of her occupation. She wouldn't have to give it up completely to go with him. She could cook and compile her cookbooks wherever she had a stove and a typewriter, but if anything exciting came up, like the series of programs for

211

television, she wouldn't be on instant call. It was irrelevant that she had already decided that her future didn't lie in television, the point was that she would have to adapt her life around his, fit in with his commitments and the conditions of his job.

It wouldn't have mattered one bit to her, and she would gladly have given up everything if it was asked of her—in the right way! The work she had been so totally and joyfully immersed in before Cliff reappeared in her life was no longer the be all and end all of her existence. But she had worked too hard at forging a career for herself for it to be dismissed lightly. She wasn't going to jeopardize it to such a degree—to any degree—for a bigoted man with only his own self-interest at heart.

She rounded on him. 'I want you to want *me*, not just my body. I'm a person, I want to be respected as such. I won't just be an object that you can sate your selfish lust on. I want a proper proposal, not that sniveling moan, "All right, I'll marry you." Well, *I* won't marry *you*! The proposal I accept will be one I can be proud of, one I'll want to remember all my life.'

'Do you know what you want, I wonder? First you want marriage, then you don't. I've made enough of a spectacle of myself as it is. My pride has to be considered, too. And I'm not proud of showing how weak I am where you're concerned. The line has got to be drawn somewhere.'

'Is that all you've got to say?'

'Every last word.'

Even then, she longed to throw herself into his arms and touch her lips to the unyielding harshness of his mouth. She had to make herself walk away from him and go upstairs to pack. Her hands obeyed her brain's instructions, but her heart wasn't in it.

This would be the second time she had walked out on a man. She had got over Jarvis in a relatively short time, but she knew she wouldn't ever get over Cliff. Was she too exacting? She was accusing Cliff of wanting everything his own way, but in one respect she was no better herself. He'd asked her to marry him! Wasn't that a miracle in itself? Did she have to lay down the law and insist on the proposal's being worded in a different way? Cliff might think that if he conceded, it would set a precedent, and he would be saddling himself with a bossy wife. Why couldn't she have said yes? If she had, she would be in Cliff's arms at that very moment instead of packing to go. She didn't want to go. And what if Cliff *had* backed down? If he'd groveled at her feet and told her all the things she wanted to hear and pleaded with her to marry him, would she have been any better suited? About the sweet things, yes, even if they weren't whole truths. A lie, if repeated often enough, seemed like the truth, and perhaps she could have made it true in time. But the groveling part wouldn't have appealed to her at all. She wouldn't want to humble Cliff. But that was what she had been trying to do.

He had been anti-marriage for so long, what had made him finally come round? She was remembering Cliff's words of comfort the time she broke down and admitted her guilt over taking Aunt Miranda for granted while she was alive and not appreciating her enough. 'Love is taking someone for granted. It's knowing without being told. The words are just the frosting on the cake,' he'd said. If Cliff were to be believed at the moment, he had proposed because he lusted for her body, and if marriage was the only way he could get it, then okay. She had taken offense at that, refusing him on the grounds of needing to be wanted for herself as a person and not just for her body. She had considered him bigoted and egotistical. A bigot was a person who holds steadfastly to an unreasonable opinion. Well, the opinions that she held dear and that seemed reasonable to her were unreasonable to him. So didn't that make her a bigot in his eyes? And egotistical. Wasn't it egotistical of her to *believe* that her body was such a turn-on, so fantastic that a man would throw away the set ideas of a lifetime to have it? She wasn't that conceited, surely? She wasn't conceited at all about her body. It was quite nice, but she would have said it was only average on sex appeal. Instead of being insulted, she ought to have been flattered that someone as superb as Cliff looked at her in that way and was prepared to go to such lengths to get her—if that was all it was.

But of course it wasn't! It wasn't possible to divorce the person from the body, and if Cliff wanted her, it meant that he wanted her for herself, which was all *she* really wanted. Love was a word that was bandied about a lot, but what did it mean? It meant having a deep affection for someone, and tender feelings.

Cliff had shown tender feelings for her the night she went to his bed and he refused to take advantage of the impulse that had taken her there. He had shown tender feelings when he'd been waiting for her to come home with her slippers warming. Who needed the icing? Cliff might not know it himself, but what had really trapped him was that tender feeling called love. It had bent even his will of iron.

With that, lots of other thoughts came flooding in, things she hadn't exactly been wrong about, but which she hadn't been right about, either, because again she had been guilty of what she was accusing him of: looking at the situation with a biased viewpoint. Things like: *he* would have to play host to *her* friends. She didn't get a chance to list any more in her mind because a prickly feeling at the back of her neck told her that Cliff was standing at the door, watching her.

She turned to look at him, and he said, 'Save yourself the trouble of packing any more things. I intend to tip the lot out. You're not going anywhere.'

'I've already decided that for myself. If you'd used your eyes properly, you'd see that I've started to take out the things I'd packed.'

'Because it dawned on you that it would be insane to drive with the roads the way they are?'

'No. It would have been, but that isn't the reason. As soon as I was composed enough, I was coming down to ask you what the conversation we've just had was all about.'

'I'm hanged if I know. I guess it all boils down to the fact that I didn't handle things too well. You're right. It was a pretty miserable proposal. I'm willing to have another go.'

She wouldn't let him climb down any further than that. Instead, she would try to measure up to him. 'It isn't necessary. I've been very stupid. If the offer is still open, yes, please, I want to marry you very much.'

\*     \*     \*

She hadn't imagined that life could be so beautiful. She had to drag herself from Cliff's side to return to the television studio for the final recording. He had taken it phlegmatically when she told him about that, declaring that

216

he wasn't surprised—hadn't he previously stated that he wasn't surprised at anything she did? 'Of course, some surprises are better than others,' he said, the dark gleam in his eye leaving her in no doubt about which surprise he was referring to. 'The best Christmas present I *almost* received,' he joked. But his voice was serious as he went on, 'You're the best thing that ever happened to me, and I could so easily have lost you through my cussedness.'

'*My* cussedness,' she insisted.

'All right, *our* cussedness. What I'm trying to say is, if you think you've got a career in television, it's okay by me.'

'What does "okay by me" mean?'

'It means I'm not overjoyed at the idea of having a wife on television. I don't want to share you, but if it's what you want, I'll put up with it.'

She thought how different his attitude was from Jarvis's.

'It isn't what I want. My ambition is to be with you.'

*     *     *

She shed tears when she got news of Edward Banks—but they were tears of gladness. He was responding to the treatment he was having. Cliff went with her to visit him in hospital, but Hannah was there, and Edward

217

had eyes for no one else. Ros had high hopes of something coming of that. If their obvious affection for each other didn't result in another wedding, she would be very disappointed.

Sometimes, on waking, she'd catch her breath on the horrible fear that it hadn't happened, that it had all been a dream. The arm possessively round her waist was solid reassurance that it was true. Slowly, she would turn her head and look into the dark eyes of the man responsible for her permanent state of exalted happiness. No man had a more contented or happier wife. The gentle ardor with which he carried her into the throbbing heat of passion never failed to amaze her. He took her body into tender keeping and led her into rapture. She'd had an idea that it would be good between them, but it surpassed everything she had hoped for, and it was getting better all the time.

She felt very humble, undeserving of all that bliss. And she loved him so much that it hurt. Usually, he was the first to wake, but one morning, a few weeks after their marriage, she was waiting for his eyes to open, the question on her lips in keeping with the last thing he had told her before she went to sleep.

'When did you first realize you loved me? Something must have triggered it off. What was it?'

'I'm not quite sure, but this might have had

something to do with it.' He reached out to the bedside table for his wallet, and from it he extracted the joke slip that had come out of the Christmas cracker about the girl getting to kiss a lot of frogs in her search for her prince.

She gasped. 'I meant to pick that up and save it as a memento. You got to it first.'

'Didn't I just! And it burned a hole in my wallet. Wouldn't give me a moment's peace or respite.'

She was touched that they had shared the same romantic impulse, even though she wasn't sure what he meant. 'I don't understand. Was it because when it was so horrible between us, when we were quarreling, or icy and distant, it reminded you of the wonderful time we had together?'

His fingers caressed her midriff, releasing tiny bubbles of joy just below the surface of her skin, bubbles that burst to wrap her in an iridescent glow. A teasing smile came to his mouth. 'No. For thinking of you kissing all the other frogs.'

'Oh, Cliff!' She giggled.

'If anyone got to kiss you, I wanted it to be me.'

Her lips lifted in confident anticipation. The sweet, fierce passion in his eyes warmed her as his tender hands brought her closer and his mouth lowered to possess hers in a long, clinging kiss.